D0373643

THE SAMURAI'S TALE

Also by Erik Christian Haugaard

Hakon of Rogen's Saga
The Little Fishes
Orphans of the Wind
A Slave's Tale
A Messenger for Parliament
Cromwell's Boy
Chase Me, Catch Nobody!
Leif the Unlucky
A Boy's Will

THE SAMURAI'S TALE

Erik Christian Haugaard

Houghton Mifflin Company
Boston

www.houghtonmifflinbooks.com

Library of Congress Cataloging-in-Publication Data
Haugaard, Erik Christian.
The samurai's tale.
Summary: In turbulent sixteenth-century Japan, orphaned Taro is taken in by a general serving the great warlord Takeda Shingen and grows up to become a samurai fighting for the enemies of his dead family.
Japan—History—Period of civil wars, 1480–1603—Juvenile fiction.
[1. Japan—History—Period of civil wars, 1480–1603—Fiction.
2. Samurai—Fiction.]
Title.
PAP ISBN 0-618-61512-1
PZ7.H286Sam 1984 [Fic] 83-22746

PAP ISBN-13: 978-0618-61512-4

Manufactured in the United States of America
DOC 15 14 13 12
4500382328

For my friend, Kazuo Inukai

Contents

List of Characters

Lord Akiyama Nobutomo *One of Lord Takeda Shingen's generals, Taro's master and friend.*

Lord Akiyama Nobutora *Father of Lord Akiyama Nobutomo.*

Lord Oda Nobunaga *Lord Takeda Shingen's rival and enemy, well known for his merciless cruelty.*

Lord Oda Nobutada *Son of Oda Nobunaga and general in his army.*

Lord Takeda Katsuyori *Son of Lord Shingen, sometimes referred to as the Wakatono, the prince.*

Lord Takeda Shingen *The Oyakata-sama, the lord of Kai, a ruthless warlord whose ambition is to conquer and rule Japan.*

Lord Takeda Yoshinobu *Son of Lord Shingen. He revolts against his father and is killed.*

Taro (Murakami Harutomo) *The hero of the story, the son of a poor samurai who died in battle.*

Togan *A lowly servant of Lord Akiyama. He befriends Taro as a child.*

Lord Tokugawa Ieyasu *A warlord who supports Oda Nobunaga. Later he becomes Shogun and ruler of Japan.*

Lord Uesugi Kenshin *Warlord and enemy of Lord Takeda Shingen.*

Wada Kansuke *Samurai, master of the Konidatai.*

Yoichi *Taro's servant.*

Yoshitoki *A young samurai, Taro's friend.*

Lord Zakoji *A retainer of Lord Akiyama, the father of Aki-hime.*

Zakoji Aki-hime *A young girl of noble blood, whom Taro loves.*

Acknowledgments

In 1981, thanks to a very generous fellowship from the Japan Foundation, I was able to spend one year in Kofu studying the Takeda family, who ruled the province of Kai in the sixteenth century. The Takedas were a fascinating clan, sometimes combining the talents of an artist, a poet, and a warrior in one person. Takeda Shingen was the most famous of this family of warlords. He fought bravely to become ruler of Japan and was finally defeated, not by his enemies but by fate. The province of Kai is now called Yamanashi, and the name of the city of Kofuchu has been shortened to Kofu. The Prefecture of Yamanashi was extraordinarily helpful to me during my stay, for which I am indeed grateful.

In spite of the generosity of these two institutions, no book would have come out of my stay without the assistance of Kazuo Inukai, to whom I dedicate this book. Professor Inukai and a band of loyal friends made my study their own as well, and gave of their time so freely that they have left me deeply indebted to them. Without their guidance and friendship I would never have understood enough of that turbulent period of Japanese history to have dared to write even the first chapter. I sincerely hope that *The Samurai's Tale* will not disappoint them; if it does, the fault will be mine.

My thanks to them all: to the Inukai family — Kazuo, Michiko, Chizumi, and Iwana — and to Motoki Fujimaki,

Nobuyoshi Aoki, Masako Taira, Noriko Ando, Ako Michiwaki, Kimie Kusumoto, Mizuhito Kanehara, Akihiko Yamagata, Chieko Hanawa, Hirofumi Matsumoto, Shigeyuki Ichimura, and Masanori Akazawa.

E.C.H.
March 1983

Preface

How should I begin my story? The storyteller is like a wanderer at the crossroad who does not know which path to follow, yet is aware that should he choose the wrong one he will never reach home. The way a story is told is as important as the tale itself, and this thought has kept me from dipping my brush in ink.

Today as I went for my usual walk outside my village, I came across a farmer plowing his field. The ox that dragged the plow was large and I paused to admire the beast. The farmer's daughter, a little girl no more than ten years old, was leading the animal. Being too frightened of the ox to take hold of its halter, she had instead attached a stick to it, which she held gingerly in her hand. When she had to help turn the giant beast at the end of a furrow her fear became so obvious that I could not help smiling. It was then that the thought came to me, not only how I should tell my story, but also, that those three — child, beast, and man plowing — were eternal; age and death could not touch them. The great lords with their armies, the knights, the samurai with their swords were the froth on the waves, the scum, the foam, the bubbles that rise and burst and are gone.

Now I know which path I must follow. I must tell my tale so simply that that man whom I watched plowing and his little frightened daughter would understand it. For they will always be with us. As long as the fiery dragon sails across our skies, men will plow their fields, and their wives and daughters will plant the rice that feeds all men, however high or low their stations.

I lived during a time when the word *peace* had little meaning, when the great lords of Japan fought over that country like dogs over a bone. A time when blood flowed like rivers and no man knew at sunrise if he would be alive when the sun set. A world filled with treachery and hate, tortured by the vanity of men who wished to rule over others before they had learned to master themselves.

I was born in the borderland between the provinces of Shinano and Echigo. My father wore the two swords of a samurai; he was a vassal of the lord of Echigo, Uesugi Kenshin. He was not wealthy but a samurai who, when needed, had helped to till his own land. He died when I was four years old, killed while serving his master in a battle against the mighty lord of Kai, Takeda Shingen.

I shall begin my tale on that day when I lost not only my father, but my mother and my two older brothers as well. A storm swept our land and when it had passed I was the only survivor of my family. In the morning of that day my name had been Murakami; I was a bushi, a knight's son whom every woman in the village would fondle and spoil. Before the sun set I had been given the name "Taro," a servant's name, and I was of no more importance than that name implied.

THE SAMURAI'S TALE

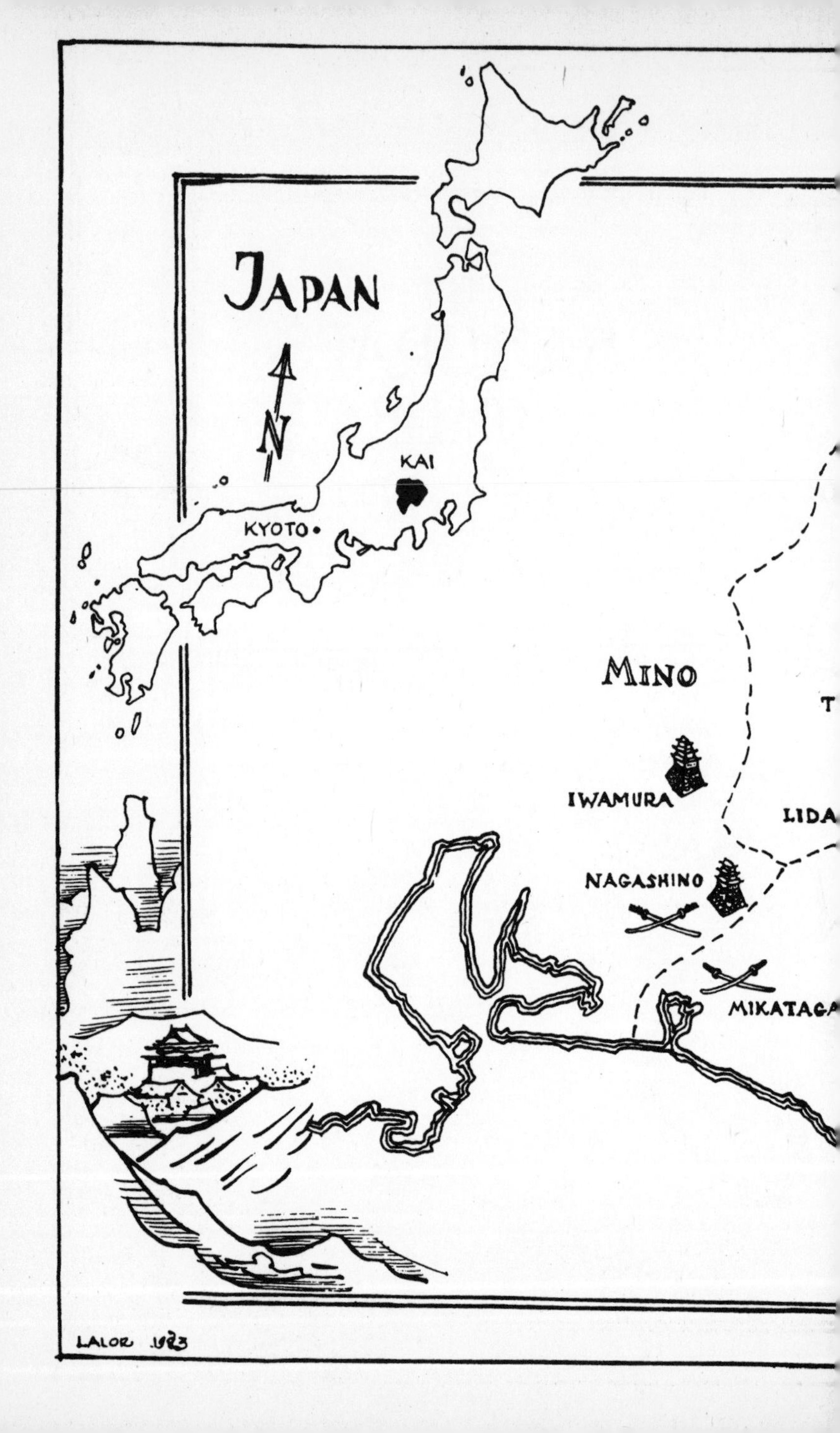
JAPAN
N
KAI
KYOTO
MINO
IWAMURA
NAGASHINO
LALOR 1923

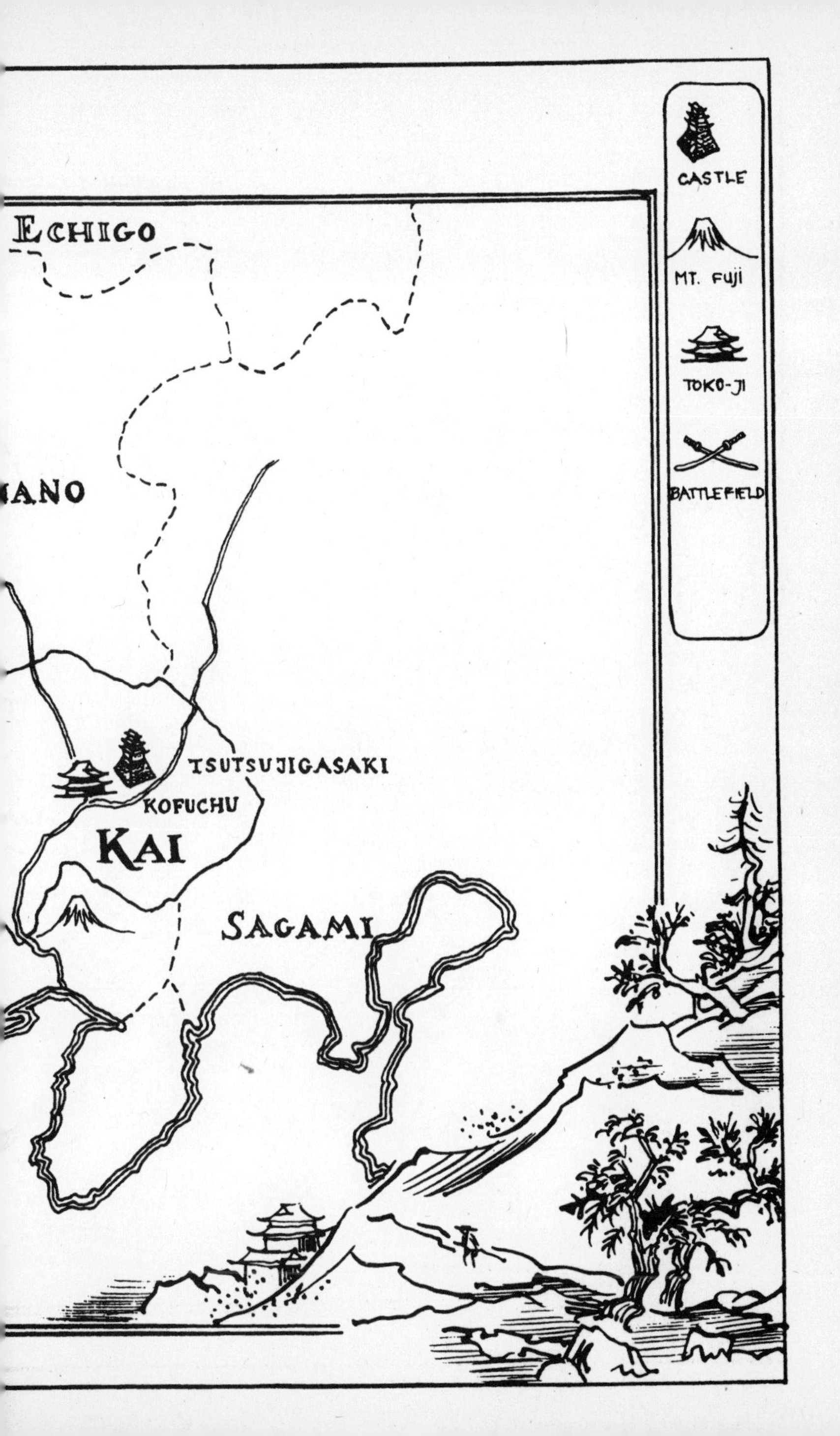

CASTLE
MT. FUJI
TOKO-JI
BATTLEFIELD
ECHIGO
NANO
TSUTSUJIGASAKI
KOFUCHU
KAI
SAGAMI

{1}

In Blood We Are All Born

"Stand still, my child." My mother's voice was harsh as she tried to hide its trembling. She was undressing me and it was the middle of the day, not a time for sleeping. "Go, girl, and put on your oldest clothes. Should they be patched so much the better," she instructed her little maid, Yone, who looked as pale and frightened as if she had seen a ghost.

"I won't wear that!" I protested, holding out my arms in a manner that made it difficult for my mother to dress me in the coarse costume she held in her hands. I knew whose clothes they were; they had belonged to the son of the man who tended my father's horses. "They smell and they are too big for me," I wailed.

My mother, who had been kneeling in front of me, let the clothes drop to the floor; it was only then I noticed that she was crying. I tried to comfort her but, almost angrily, she pushed me away.

"You will have to wear them," she declared, holding up the clothes again, and this time I allowed her to dress me in them. I have often tried to guess, as a grown man, whom her tears were for. Then I thought they were for me, but a child's world is so small that it is easy for him to think himself the center of it. My mother had just learned of her husband's death — a friend of his had galloped through the village spreading the news of Uesugi Kenshin's defeat and of my father's fate. Were these tears for his sake, or were they for her own? Before he had fled onward the rider had also told that a large part of Lord Takeda's army was on its way and would be in our village soon. She must have known what awaited her, for Takeda Shingen was ruthless towards those whom he considered his enemies. My oldest brother was eight years old and he had been born when my mother was sixteen. She was still very young to face death.

"There!" My mother pushed me gently away to have a look at me. "You are still a handsome little boy," she said and smiled while she drew me close to her again. Just at that moment Yone returned and my mother beckoned to her to come and stand beside me. Then, standing up, she scrutinized the two of us and shook her head.

"I am going to hide you over in the kura," she said, "and you must stay there and not be frightened."

The kura was the storehouse that lay behind our house, where my father kept rice and other things of value; it was usually locked and I was not allowed to play in there.

"If they find you, say that he is your little brother." My mother looked severely at Yone, who nodded her head submissively.

"But I am not her little brother!" I objected, not liking any of what was happening to me.

"We are only pretending." My mother glanced at me for a moment but then turned her attention to the girl. "Stay where I put you until morning; then, if the soldiers have gone, make your way to Arai." At the mention of the place where she was born, one large tear ran down my mother's cheek, but she brushed it away angrily as if that single tear had betrayed her. "Come!" she commanded and led the way towards the storehouse.

When I think of it now, her plan must have been born out of desperation, for surely the storehouse was a poor hiding-place. It would not be left untouched. Neither had she chosen a very wise companion for me, for Yone was a foolish girl who would never have found her way to distant Arai.

"You stay inside this chest — don't come out whatever happens." My mother had opened the lid of a large wooden chest that had contained all her earthly possessions when my father had married her and brought her from her parents' house in Arai. The lid had split in several places and the chest had been deemed not good enough for the house. "Come." My mother lifted me up and for a moment she pressed me against her in one last caress, then she dropped me into the chest. "Take care of him!" she admonished Yone as she closed the lid.

I sat completely still, the musty odor of rice all around me. I was not scared. I could hear Yone's breathing but there was another sound as well; she was crying. Girls cry easily, I thought, even when they are as big as Yone. I hardly ever cried, only if I had fallen and hurt myself badly, but Yone had not fallen.

It seemed to me that it was long since my mother had left when I heard the sound of horses. Then came the shouts of many men and a great deal of noise and suddenly, in a momentary stillness, the scream of a woman. Yone, who had difficulty sitting upright in the chest, had moved very close to me. I could smell her. I liked the smell of women better than that of men and best of all I liked the smell of my mother when she had just bathed and put on perfume. Then I would climb as close to her as I could. Sometimes this would annoy her and she would call one of her women to come and take me away. Somebody banged on the door of the kura but the storehouse doors were solid. Yone had moved so close to me that she put her arms around me and hugged me; she was shaking and that surprised me for it was not cold at all.

The men who had been banging on the door of the kura had gone away, but now they were back and this time they were breaking the lock. That was the first moment when I felt any fear at all; before it had all been like a game that my mother and I were playing. But somehow the sound of the hammer hitting the lock made me realize that what was happening was terribly, terribly serious.

"They will kill us," Yone whispered in my ear and sniffed in an effort to control her tears. But as she heard the lock break and the door of the kura swing open she gave up all hope of stemming them and wailed, as if she felt a knife on her throat already, "I don't want to die!"

"What have we here?" a gruff voice asked as the lid of the chest was thrown open. "Come out!" the voice commanded. At the same time two hands grabbed our ears and dragged us forth. The soldier looked us over for a moment, as though debating within himself if he should kill us. So many had died that day that a child and a servant girl more would make little difference. But maybe he was tired of killing — even that can become wearisome — for he did not draw his sword but instead indicated by a movement of his head that we were to follow him.

The yard behind the house was filled with soldiers, some lying down resting, others having their wounds attended to. I needed no urging but ran towards the house, expecting to find my mother. She was there, lying in a pool of blood, dead! I recognized her kimono first, though it was one she seldom wore. It was the only one of silk she owned. She must have dressed herself in it after she had hidden Yone and me. Beside her lay the lifeless bodies of my two brothers and, near the entrance to the room, two women who had served my mother. I know that it may seem unnatural that I did not scream or even cry at the sight, but I did not, and that probably saved my life.

"Who are they?"

I turned in the direction of the voice. A stout, powerful-looking man dressed in armor, his helmet lying beside him, was drinking tea together with another officer, who was dressed in blue and wearing a white scarf.

"I found them hiding in a chest," the soldier, who was standing right behind us, explained.

"He is my little brother," Yone wailed.

"You are lying," the stout man declared matter-of-factly, and Yone obediently nodded her head. "Who is he?"

"The master's youngest," an old servant woman, who

had been with my father since he was a child, answered in a mournful voice. It was she who had prepared the tea the two men were drinking.

"Three sons! He was a lucky man," the stout officer declared.

"Until today." The man dressed in blue smiled and then, turning to the soldier, he asked, "How much rice was there in the storehouse?"

"More than fifty horses can carry."

This news seemed to please both men, for they smiled. In my father's kura was stored not only his own rice, but also rice he had collected in taxes for his master the lord of Echigo, Uesugi Kenshin.

One of the men nodded his head in my direction while he glanced significantly at the soldier and, though I was not yet five years old, I understood the meaning of that silent command. I leapt toward the corner of the room where I kept a bamboo sword my father had given me. Once I held it in my hand I turned toward the soldier in an attitude of defense.

This act of mine made both the officers laugh, the stout one so much that he shook. Not knowing what to do next, the soldier stood hesitantly, waiting for further command.

"He is truly the son of a samurai," the officer dressed in blue exclaimed.

"Akiyama!" The stout officer nodded towards me. "Catch him and I will make you a present of him."

The officer Akiyama stood up and, glancing at me with a look used to obedience, he said, "Come here, boy!"

For a moment I hesitated, but then decided that he meant me no harm. Putting down my bamboo sword I walked up to him, keeping my gaze on his face.

"What is your name?" he asked.

"Murakami," I replied, using my family name.

"You can have him, but not as Murakami," the stout officer interrupted and then turning to me he said, "If you want to keep that name, you shan't keep your head." He looked down at his sword as if he contemplated drawing it.

"I shall call him 'Taro.'" The samurai Akiyama grinned. "He can take care of my horses when he grows up." He drew me close to him for a moment. I think he suspected that I might claim my right to my family name even though this could mean losing my head, for I had more pride than sense.

"Go, girl, and take the boy with you. Wait for me outside," he ordered Yone, who was near fainting with fright. He dismissed the soldier at the same time.

"That was Takeda Shingen, the greatest and most powerful lord in all of Japan," the soldier declared with awe in his voice, at the same time turning over in his mind his own behavior and wondering if it had been fitting.

"And who was the other one?" I asked as I sat down on the wooden steps leading to my parents' house.

"A great captain, the lord of Akiyama. Nobutomo is his name. You are a fortunate boy to become his servant."

"Why would he not let me keep my own name?" I asked.

"Oh, if he did that you might some day claim your right to this place." The soldier looked around, as though wondering which of the samurai who had helped Lord Takeda to victory would be rewarded with my father's house.

"It is always best to kill the whole family of your enemies and leave no-one about." The soldier nodded sagely.

"Why did they kill the two women who attended my lady?" Yone's voice still shook, but she was not crying anymore.

"Out of respect for the lad's mother, I suspect." The soldier had lost interest in us and, seeing a friend, he left, admonishing us first to stay where we were.

There we sat, the serving maid Yone and the servant lad Taro, until the sun set. Then we were given some watery millet gruel to eat and were shown a place in a shed where we might sleep for the night. The evening before, my mother had undressed me and I had slept beside her under the same soft covers. That night my resting place was more fitting as the kennel for a dog.

{2}

The Journey to Kofuchu

On the rough walls of the shed two flies were running up and down as if there were a purpose to their wandering. I had been watching them, wondering why they did not fall down, and thinking that one of them was I and the other fly was Yone. It was early morning, and though the sun had already risen I guessed it still to be the hour of the tiger. I had been awake long, listening to the noises from outside. Some soldiers had already left. I had heard the sound of their horses' hoofs as the riders made the animals canter. Now the flies were in the air, circling above my head; how nice if one were able to fly! Then my mother and I could have flown away yesterday, and she would still be alive.

Lying as close to me as she could, Yone was snoring, her mouth a little open. I thought how much prettier my mother had looked when sleeping. One of the flies landed on her nose and began to polish its wings with its legs. Yone sniffed in annoyance; the fly stopped its morning toilet and flew away. Just then there was a sudden sound from outside and the girl woke with a little scream. As she sat up and saw me she covered her mouth with her hand.

"I am hungry!" I said, a demand that had always resulted in food being brought to me. Yone looked in fear towards the door that hid and protected us from the dangers outside. I repeated my command, for I was still the bushi's son and she my little servant.

Yone pulled the door ajar and looked outside. I too wanted to see but she pushed me aside.

"You stay here, and don't make any noise," she admonished. To my surprise, she was talking to me as if I were indeed her younger brother. Then, before I had time to object, she had slipped outside and closed the door behind her.

As soon as Yone was gone I wished I had not asked for food and sent her away. Once left alone I grew frightened and all that had happened yesterday became real again. Two of the boards in the wall did not fit together and left a slit I could look through. The yard at the back of our house was still filled with soldiers. They were poor farmers who had to follow the samurai who was their master. None that I could see wore the swords of a samurai. This made me less fearful, thinking them too mean to have any rights over me.

Yone returned with a bowl of the same millet gruel that had served as our dinner the night before. But she was not alone; the soldier who had discovered and dragged us from our hiding-place was with her. I was sitting on the floor when they entered. The soldier looked down at me with disgust, for he had been told to keep an eye on us until we came to the castle of Takeda Shingen at Kofuchu. Suddenly he grinned and pointed to my feet. I was still wearing a pair of soft deerskin shoes. When my mother had dressed me in rags she had either forgotten or simply had not had the heart to take my shoes away.

"Take them off!" the soldier commanded and I obeyed, even handing them to him when he stretched out his hand.

"I have a son your age. They will fit him." The soldier laughed, then spying the two flies on the wall he lifted one of the shoes and swatted. Recalling that I had named one of the flies Yone and the other after myself, I wondered which one had been killed.

"My feet hurt," I complained to Yone but she, having walked barefoot through the twelve years of her life, did not care.

"I can't walk any farther. You carry me," I suggested.

"You walk!" Yone did not even cast me a glance, she was looking ahead at the long row of packhorses, but then she held out her hand.

"I couldn't carry you. You are too heavy," she said and, smiling with a grown-up's cunning, she added, "You are much too big to be carried."

At the crossing of a stream we halted to give both animals and men a chance to drink and rest, but not nearly long enough to suit me. It was fall, the rice had been harvested several weeks before, and now the nights were cold in the mountains. The soldiers were eager to press forward, hoping either to find shelter for the night or to reach the great level plain of Kai. They had already spent two nights shivering around fires in the mountains.

"Look!" I pointed to my feet; a stone had cut the skin and the gash was still bleeding.

"Put your feet in the water, boy. That will stop the bleeding."

I looked up. Instead of Yone it was the soldier who was standing behind me. Dutifully I obeyed; the water was not yet winter cold, and it felt pleasant on my weary feet.

"Would you like to ride?" the soldier asked. "You are not used to going barefoot."

"Thank you." I nodded, saying yes to both. One of the horses carried only half a load of rice and, for the rest of that day, I was allowed to sit astride it. That was my first time on horseback, for I had been deemed too young to ride even the oldest and most docile of my father's mares.

That night we reached the foothills of that great valley, crossed by two rivers, where Takeda Shingen's residence, Tsutsujigasaki Castle, stood.

My father's village was located in a narrow dale with few ricefields, and he had numbered the people he reigned over in hundreds. As we made our way across the great plain, it surprised me that the world contained so many people. Ricefields there were in plenty and all of them much larger than the ones in my poor mountain home. We came to toll-gates where ordinary travelers had to pay in order to pass, but we, carrying Lord Shingen's rice, had no need to. The men guarding the gates saluted us, and having heard of the great victory, they shouted words of encouragement while they greedily counted the horses to find out how many kokus of rice we were carrying.

On the fourth day of our journey we entered Kofuchu. This was no village, but a proper town. Here were strange sights to stare at enough to please anyone. On the outskirts of the town lived the poor, in houses that were mere hovels, meaner than any in our village. From here a band of ragged children escorted us until they annoyed the soldiers so much that they shooed them away, giving them a few raps over their bare legs with the sticks that they had been using on the horses. The children frightened both Yone and me a little, they were so different from the children we were used to. They did not seem the least bit scared of the soldiers; one of them even laughed when he was hit.

One of the soldiers took great pleasure in dealing out this punishment, darting in among the children and hitting them as hard as he could. He was a man older than the rest, but his age had gained him no respect, for the others treated him with contempt. During our journey he had shown himself no friend to me, taking delight in reminding me of the fate of my parents. Once while we were eating and Yone held a bowl of rice gruel in her hands, he had pushed her so that she spilled it. He laughed, but the other soldiers did not share his mirth and one of them gave Yone some of his gruel.

As we passed by the entrance of the Takeda Castle this soldier left his horse and, grabbing me by my shoulder, he pointed to something on the wall.

"Bow to your father!" he shouted. I looked in the direction he indicated. There on stakes were the heads of human beings. Taking hold of mine he forced me to bow towards these grisly relics.

"Let the boy be!" the soldier who had been put in charge of me shouted.

"I am just teaching him respect for his parents!" My tormentor grinned but let go of me. I ran to the soldier whom I had learned to consider my protector.

"You let the boy be, or I shall put your head up among the rest of them," he shouted at the older soldier. "Get back to your horse!" he commanded.

Making a face as he obeyed, the bully returned to his horse, which had broken rank and was walking ahead of the rest.

"Those are the heads of bandits captured many weeks ago," the soldier explained, pointing in the direction of the trophies on the wall. "Keep far away from that man, there is little good in him," he advised. "He is a wasp in autumn. He stings without reason."

After the rice had been unloaded in a storehouse and the horses taken to a field and turned loose, our guide told us that he would take us to the mansion of Akiyama Nobutomo.

On the way there we passed a group of boys more richly dressed than I had ever seen even grown-ups. One of them had boots with fur showing at their tops. I think I noticed those particularly because my own feet were bare.

"Who are they?" I asked.

"The one with the sword was the Wakatono, Lord

Shingen's son." The soldier made a grimace, not altogether complimentary. "For him you cannot bow low enough and, if he should kick you, remember to thank him."

I looked back. The boy with the fur-lined boots also wore a sword. He could not have been much more than ten years old, I thought.

"Where are we going?" Yone asked as the soldier led us down a narrow alley.

"I had orders to hand you over to someone in the cookhouse." Our guide laughed. "Did you expect Lord Akiyama to come in person to receive you?"

"He said I was supposed to take care of his horses," I complained, feeling that the kitchen was not a fit place for a samurai's son.

"That might be so. But I think he wants you to grow a little first." The soldier had stopped in front of a mean-looking building. Beyond some trees I could see the roof of a much larger house. "Those who work in the cookhouse are always well-fed, while the stable-boys are, as often as not, hungrier than the horses."

The soldier shouted a name and a little while later a door was opened slightly. An enormous head appeared, blinking its eyes as if the man it belonged to had just been awakened.

"Lord Akiyama told me to bring these two here." The soldier grinned. He was happy to hand us over to someone else.

"I suppose we could roast the little one and make soup of the big one!" The man opened the door wider; to my surprise it was only his head that was so big; the body it belonged to was of no great size.

"Boil them or roast them, it is all the same to me!" With a wave of his hand the soldier turned on his heel and left.

"Come!" Opening the door fully, the man made a motion to shoo us inside.

I looked at Yone. I knew she was frightened, but she obeyed and I followed her into the dark room beyond.

{3}

The "Dog" Taro

Shortly after my arrival in Lord Akiyama's mansion, or rather in the shed that housed one of his cooks, Yone disappeared out of my life. One day she was not there anymore; she was my last link with my parents and my former life, but I recall no pains when it snapped. I had made new friends and had no need of her anymore.

In everyone's life there are certain people who have helped to form his character and given a direction to his life; they are like big stones in a river that force the water to alter its course. Lord Akiyama's cook was such a stone in the little stream of my early life. He was known as Togan by everyone. He had received that nickname because of the size and shape of his head, which, I must admit, did resemble a melon.

He did not seem to mind being called by that name and answered to it as if it brought him honor rather than ridicule. Perhaps for that reason most people seemed to have forgotten its original meaning and meant no harm at all when they called him by it. I recall once asking him if he did not mind. He looked at me in surprise and then, feeling the shape of his head with both hands, he said, "But, Taro, it is like a melon."

Togan did not cook for Lord Akiyama. His household had a more skillful cook whose kitchen was far away from where Togan reigned. He cooked for the servants — the gardeners, the stable-boys, and all those in so lowly a position that they were more used to millet and barley than to rice.

Lord Akiyama had many retainers. Some were of such importance that they ate in his mansion; others took their meals in other houses in the grounds; the lowliest of all — among whom I belonged — ate in the kitchen where Togan was cook. Even the stable-boys had a room of their own, and I often brought their food to them there. Each person within the grounds of the mansion knew exactly what his position was, its importance and the amount of respect he could demand from those beneath him. I was spared having to speculate over this since everyone was above me and, if I should be in doubt about the degree of respect a person deserved, I quickly learned that humility in very large portions was always consumed with the greatest of pleasure.

An exception to this rule was Togan, who disliked seeing anyone demean himself. He treated all with exactly the same degree of politeness. Even to me, though he made me work hard, he never gave an order without adding a please and a thank you, dropped as naturally from his lips to me as to a samurai.

"Impoliteness, Taro," he would say, "marks you as a fool, for it takes away from you an advantage and gives you none in return. On the other hand, excessive meekness and modesty may make others distrust you and suspect you of being a schemer not worthy of their confidence."

There are many jobs in a kitchen that even a small child can perform. Because of Togan I found few of them irksome; he taught me that there was no work not worth doing well. He was full of truly wise sayings, and if I did not understand them he did not mind spending the time explaining what he meant. He could read, which few of Lord Akiyama's servants could, and wrote a very forceful hand. He was a fervent Buddhist and practiced Zen, but he never went to the temple. He used to visit a priest who lodged near the temple. Sometimes he would sit for hours facing the wall, staring at it as if he were trying his best to look right through it. But then suddenly he would stop and take out his bamboo flute and play. I liked to listen to him, especially in the summer evenings, when we would sprawl under a great pine tree growing near our shed until late into the night. Togan said that the tree was holy and that a god lived in it. Declaring that he had seen it himself, he claimed that the god was about my size and had hair as green as the needles on the tree. He would tell such tales while looking at me so seriously that I did not for a moment doubt what he was saying. I used to search for the little god of the pine tree, thinking him just the right size for me. Once Togan gave me his flute to play, but I could make no sound come out of it even though I blew as hard as I could. He laughed and promised me that when I had grown a little he would teach me how to play and make me a flute of my own.

Togan's flutes were highly valued, though he never charged more than a few coppers for them. He would take great care in making them, selecting bamboo of the right thickness and quality, which could easily take a whole afternoon. He loved making the flutes and the payment he asked for was meant to spare the purchaser the embarrassment of receiving a gift. But he would not make a flute for everyone; for those he refused he had such a long list of excuses that he tired them out before he offended them.

Those years I spent with Togan were probably the happiest of my life. He took better care of me than most parents would and I grew strong and straight like a well-tended young tree. The soldier who brought me to Kofuchu had been right when he claimed that a kitchen was a good place to work, for I was always well-fed and in the winter months, when the plain of Kai can be bitterly cold and the mountains that surround it are covered in snow, I was warm.

What Togan wanted to teach me, more than anything else, was contentment. As we sat under the tree in summer he would point to a bird and say, "Look, Taro, that bird is satisfied being what it is, a bird. It knows what it can do and what it can't . . . it is content, just as the tree is satisfied with being a tree. The little cloud up there" — here Togan would point towards a small cloud sailing in the sky — "knows that it is not big enough to hold thunder or rain within it, but it is not unhappy because of that."

I always agreed with him. I knew he meant me well and sometimes I was convinced that it was wrong of me to wish to be more than I was. But I could not be content as Togan wished me to be. When I saw the sons of the lord or the samurai, I had only one desire — to be among them and to be recognized as their equal.

The year that Lord Takeda's son, Shiro, came of age a great celebration was held in his honor. Shiro was the Wakatono I had seen on my first day in Kofuchu, he who had worn the fur-lined boots. Now, as he came of age, his name was changed to Takeda Suwa Katsuyori. It was my eleventh year and an archery contest was held in a field near the castle in which all the sons of the samurai who had reached manhood that year would take part. They were all splendidly dressed and each one of them had an attendant carrying a banner with the family crest on it. But Katsuyori was more splendidly dressed than all the others. Since he had an older brother his attendant carried not the banners of his father, Lord Shingen, but those of his mother's family, the Suwas, for he had been declared the heir of that family.

As I stood among the wretched urchins as poor as myself, who had been allowed to come and watch their betters, I felt so strongly that I was the equal of the splendidly dressed young people that I completely forgot my barefoot state and ragged clothing. Suddenly I walked out into the field as if I were one of the participants. A servant of Lord Akiyama who knew me grabbed me by the arm and demanded to know where I thought I was going. Getting no reply, he turned me around and gave me a push back toward my peers. Looking at them and then down at myself — it had rained that morning and my feet were very dirty — I burst out crying. Ashamed of my tears, I ran from the field home to the kitchen, to Togan.

It was spring, just after the plum trees had lost their flowers. When I came close to my master's mansion I saw a little mangy dog. Its pelt was covered with sores, and as I came near it put its tail between its legs and crouched. I kicked it angrily. It whined, but did not try to escape.

"You should bite!" I shouted at the frightened little animal, who was still cringing, waiting for further kicks. I had already raised my foot to supply them when I noticed Togan. He was standing near the lane that led down to the shed, staring at me.

My anger turned to shame as I walked toward him. He said nothing but followed me down the path. I can recall thinking, If only he would hit me, as I kicked the dog, but I knew he would not.

Finally, as we came near our home, I turned towards him and wailed, "I am like that little dog!"

Togan only smiled and shook his head.

"You are not," he said. "You are a healthy little puppy."

That evening, as Togan played for us on his flute, I thought, He is right, I am not that mangy little dog I met in the street. The dog Taro was strong and healthy, but not content with being a dog.

{4}

The Death of Togan

Death will always be part of life; it is as natural as the seasons. The hot summer will slowly glide into fall and that, in turn, into winter, when the trees stand barren and the cold snow covers the mountains. But there are those who are cursed to live in times when death seems to come out of season, when the winter of a man's life may leap upon him in the midst of summer greenness.

How young Togan was when he died I am not sure. I had then used so small a part of my life that I thought him old. I think he must have been in his mid-thirties, the noon of his life. As I have mentioned, he was not tall yet his body was big; it was his legs that were unusually short. He was strong and liked showing off his strength. This was his only vanity, but it explained his passion for wrestling, which was to cost him his life.

Near the Hoko temple, located on the narrow street called Warehouse Road, wrestling matches were sometimes held. These were not official ones that the lords and samurai attended. Here, the spectators were the riff-raff of Kofuchu, and the wrestlers themselves often poor at their sport. There would be betting on the results and sometimes a fight would break out among the rabble watching them.

News had spread that a young man from beyond the

mountains had proven such an apt wrestler that he had thrown some of the best in the province. This had tempted Togan to visit a part of the town that otherwise he never frequented. In the old Street of the Dyers, which leads to Warehouse Road, lived some of the poorest and most miserable people of Kofuchu. When the dyers had moved, these wretches made their homes in the ramshackle sheds they had left behind. Among a group of these beggars I spied one who looked like the old soldier who had plagued me when I was taken to Kofuchu. I debated whether I should say anything to Togan but decided not to, for I was not certain that it was he. Still, their presence made me uneasy, for it was obvious they all had had too much to drink. As we approached the place where the wrestling match was to be held, I felt a sense of danger that made me want to turn back.

The wrestler proved a disappointment; he was strong but not skillful. He won the first two matches, but his opponents were not true wrestlers, merely young men who wanted to test their strength. In the third match the challenger was a wrestler; although not a champion of anywhere but his own village, he threw the young man from beyond the mountains as if he were a sack of rice. Togan was annoyed, and he commented in the most derogatory fashion not only upon the match but also upon the place where it was held. I was aware that some of the people near us were taking exception to his opinions. I glanced around to see if I could find any of Lord Akiyama's servants in the crowd but saw none whom I knew.

"If this place is not to your liking why did you come?" a voice jeered at us. Togan did not reply, but motioned to me that we should leave. The group of drunkards from Old Dyers' Street barred our way, and foremost among them stood the soldier.

"Please allow us to pass," Togan asked politely, at the same time making a small bow towards the group.

"Shouldn't we make them pay a toll?" the leader of the party demanded, and I felt certain that he was the very same man who had made me bow towards the heads of the bandits. He was standing with his hands on his hips, right in front of us, making it obvious that he was not going to move. A roar of approval greeted his suggestion.

"We are poor people," Togan muttered.

"He says he is too poor!" the drunk shouted to his audience. Then, as he poked Togan in the stomach, he added, "I say he is fat-bellied."

"Please keep your hands to yourself!" Togan's voice was low and menacing. I knew that he was angry.

"He says that he does not want me to touch him!" The man turned towards his companions. "He says he is ticklish." Then suddenly his right fist shot out and hit the unsuspecting Togan in the middle of the stomach. Togan was taken completely unaware; he doubled up in pain, which made our tormentor laugh.

"That's better. Now down on your knees! You too, boy!" he ordered.

I looked at Togan, waiting to see what he would do. Suddenly I recalled what a soldier had said of this man:

"He is a wasp in autumn. He stings without reason."

Togan had straightened up and, though the blow had knocked the breath out of him, he did not look like a man who was about to fall on his knees.

"Let us pass!" Togan commanded.

"I said on your knees, fool!" The old soldier would not let us go.

"You too, boy!" he shouted as he swatted me across the face with his open hand. The blow was unexpected and so hard that I fell to the ground. As I rose slowly I felt my cheek smarting. Some of the people laughed, others jeered; they had formed a ring around us. This was better sport to them than the wrestling match had been.

"Leave the boy alone!" Togan shouted as he charged and, using his head as a battering-ram, he sent the older man sprawling on the ground. But he was up in a moment and, drawing a dagger from his sash, he attacked Togan. I saw the blade glitter twice in the sun. The second time it was stained with blood and Togan had fallen to the ground. A gasp was heard from the crowd, as if they all had drawn their breath at the same time.

I threw myself down beside Togan. Blood was flowing from two deep wounds in his chest. I put my hands on them as if that would stop the blood, but it oozed out between my fingers.

"That will teach him better manners." Togan's murderer looked triumphantly around him. Some of the crowd was leaving; the sight of the blood had sobered them.

"What is happening here?" a voice demanded. At the sound of it most of the witnesses to the deed found they had business elsewhere and disappeared.

"He attacked me, my lord." The soldier, who was now sober, bowed deeply and respectfully.

"That is not true!" I shouted angrily as I jumped to my feet. It was only then that I realized that the newcomer was Lord Akiyama, accompanied by a group of servants and retainers.

"Togan was your cook," I said, bowing at the same time.

Lord Akiyama wrinkled his brow as he tried to recall who Togan was. To help him, I explained that he had cooked for the servants. One of the men who had come with Lord Akiyama was kneeling beside Togan. I noticed that he was a samurai and, for some reason, that pleased me. He rose and whispered something to his master.

"How dare you kill one of my servants!" Lord Akiyama turned on the soldier angrily. "Who are you?" he demanded.

"I used to serve Yamamoto Kansuke. I come from Ise." The soldier accompanied this information with a sly smile. Then, as he became aware that he still held the bloody dagger in his hand, he wiped it and put it away.

"Unfortunately for you, Lord Kansuke is dead and cannot vouch for the truth of what you have said." Lord Akiyama's voice was soft as silk. "No doubt you not only come from Ise, but claim birth in Koga."

Togan's murderer looked around for his friends, but

all of them had vanished. He turned pale as he tasted the bitter savor of fear, then he dropped to his knees as he declared, "I have served Lord Takeda as well!"

"No doubt." Lord Akiyama glanced at me as he asked, "How did this happen, boy?"

"We had come to see the wrestling match. Togan had done no harm to him or anyone when he" — with a nod of my head I indicated whom I meant — "would not let us leave. He commanded us to get on our knees, and he hit Togan and me too . . . and then . . . then . . ." My voice broke and I felt shame that tears were forming in my eyes. "Then he killed Togan with his knife, even though Togan didn't have any weapon but his fists."

"An oversight on his part if he wanted to frequent places like this. . . ." Lord Akiyama looked at the soldier, who was still kneeling in front of him.

"I have always reserved my sword for those as brave as myself, or at least as honest. I would not tarnish it by doing Kai the service of removing that house of lies you carry on your shoulders. I do not believe you ever served Kansuke, or were ever one of his spies. A proper ninja is not so foolish as to engage in brawls like this."

It was well known that Lord Akiyama did not respect those samurai who were called ninjas and were spies and sometimes assassins. This distaste was shared by many of the lords and samurai, but not by the ruler of Kai, Lord Takeda Shingen. It was well known that the Ise country, and especially the Koga district, was famous for producing these soldiers who always dressed in black —

no doubt to honor their accomplice, Night, or their master, Death.

Suddenly one of the men accompanying Lord Akiyama stepped forward.

"I know the man, my lord," he said with disdain. "It is true that he served Lord Kansuke. He was his servant but ran away, taking some of his master's money with him — this he forgot to mention."

"An oversight caused by modesty, no doubt." Lord Akiyama made a motion with his hand, a signal for his retainers to remove the thief. Knowing only too well what fate awaited him, Togan's murderer threw himself upon the ground, knocking his head so hard upon the earth that the rough edge of a pebble broke the skin of his forehead.

"I am innocent of that charge!" he screamed, holding up his hands in despair, begging for the succor that none would give him.

"No doubt" — Lord Akiyama's hand was pointing towards Togan, whose face had already taken on the pallor of death — "but you are guilty of this!"

Two men had grabbed the prisoner by his arms, at the same time one of them took the precaution of removing the dagger from his sash. As he was hauled upright he caught sight of me and a sudden glimmer of recognition showed on his face.

"I should have killed you when we were in the mountains!" he screamed as he was dragged away, "but you will make food for crows yet."

"And who are you, the cook's helper?" Lord Akiyama asked.

I did not answer immediately because I was watching the men who were carrying Togan.

"Boy!" This time the tone of voice was one of command. "Did you not hear me?"

"Yes, I was his helper," I mumbled and then a little louder I added, "He was my friend."

Lord Akiyama smiled. "And what did the scoundrel mean when he said he should have killed you?"

I looked at him in surprise, for I still had not realized fully that he did not remember me.

"I traveled with the rice, my lord," I replied, a little confused. "He was one of the men who led the horses."

"Led the horses, what horses?" Lord Akiyama wrinkled his brow in an effort to understand. Then, suddenly, he burst out laughing. "You are the little samurai with the bamboo sword!"

I nodded in agreement and then, gathering all my courage, I said, "And you promised me then that I should help take care of your horses."

"Did I?" His features became thoughtful but soon a smile burst forth again. "Taro, yes, that is what I called you. I remember it all now."

Lord Akiyama turned to one of his companions — a samurai dressed almost as splendidly as he was — and related the story of our first meeting. When he had finished he spoke to me again.

"Taro," he said, "I always keep my word, but you were a little too small then, or my horses too big."

"I know, my lord," I gasped, "but what about now? I have grown since then. . . ." Now that Togan was dead I wanted more than ever to escape from the kitchen.

"We shall see." Then, as Lord Akiyama noticed the despair painted on my face, he added good-naturedly as he turned to leave, "True, you have grown . . . children make a habit of doing that. . . . I think you may be the right size now."

For a moment I felt like shouting for joy, as if I had already regained my name and my birthright, instead of the mere promise of becoming a stable-boy. Then my eyes caught sight of the pools of blood that the dry earth had not yet totally absorbed and my new-found happiness turned to misery.

I went to the temple and there I washed my hands, then I fell on my knees and prayed for Togan's soul.

{5}

The Stable-boy Taro

Lord Akiyama kept his word and I was moved from the kitchen to the room where the boys and young men who kept his horses slept and lived. I was the youngest among them and, therefore, deemed fit to be their servant and the receiver of the most unpleasant jobs. If pride is a fault, I was far from flawless, and I suffered much.

A boy named Jiro proved a particularly troublesome master. He was not much older than I, and much concerned with his own dignity. I suspected that it was not long since he had filled my place as the youngest. For his own pleasure he would order me about needlessly and delight when he saw my face grow red with anger. Still I bided my time, though I suspected that sooner or later we would have to fight it out. But possibly Togan's death had taught me a little patience.

Jiro's father was a house-servant, not of Lord Akiyama but of another of Lord Takeda's generals. His master's name was Lord Obu Toramasa, by his enemies called "the wild tiger of Kofuchu." It was said that he was the most daring of Lord Takeda Shingen's officers. During the coldest time of the year, when the mountains were covered in snow, a rumor sprang up about a revolt that was to take place at any moment. Jiro dropped hints that he knew all about it, but would not tell, having been sworn to secrecy. It seemed to me that he swelled visibly during those weeks, like a frog about to lay eggs.

Suddenly, before the revolt had even taken place, it was all over. The leaders of the rebellion had been Lord Obu and Lord Takeda's eldest son, Yoshinobu. So pitifully unsuccessful had it been that you could not help but feel sorry for those who had partaken in this foolish venture. Lord Obu was not allowed to kill himself in an honorable manner; he was led to the place where common criminals were executed and there made to pay for his crime together with most of his retainers. Yoshinobu, Lord Shingen's son, was confined in Toko-ji temple, a prisoner. Lord Obu's house-servants were dispatched to the gold mines in Kurokawa, a place that no man went to by his own choice.

If Jiro had resembled a frog blown up with pride, he now looked most of all like a wet cat. Before the revolt he had often bragged about the important position his father held and even hinted that he would soon rise even higher; now there was no longer any mention of his father. The boy did not even dare leave our room, but would hide in a corner, shaking with fear, at any moment expecting to be dragged forth if not to the execution grounds, then to the mines. But as the days and weeks passed and nothing happened, he slowly regained his courage. Jiro was now like a general who has lost a battle but not the war. He felt that he had fallen in the esteem of the others and was eager to regain what prestige he had had. With the cunning of a fool, he turned on me as the easiest victim, but the other boys were not as willing as they had been to let him tyrannize me. They recalled only too well the important airs he had put on and how they had resented them.

Lord Akiyama kept only a few horses at his mansion in Kofuchu; there was not room for more than ten in the stable and it was seldom full. An hour's ride away he owned some meadowland on the banks of the river Kamanashi. The lower parts sometimes flooded in the rainy season, but it was good grazing. Here a large herd of horses was left to fend for itself. Lord Akiyama's pride, his black stallion, was kept at home, as were a few of his best breeding mares. In the district over which he was lord, he had even more horses and, in time of war, he could supply mounts for more than two hundred retainers.

One morning Jiro and I and an older boy named Matazo were sent down to the meadow to fetch three horses. We set out early in the morning; in the stables we picked up bridles and, as a matter of course, Matazo handed me his to carry. When Jiro saw this he gave me his as well. For a moment I thought of throwing the bridle down on the floor and telling him to pick it up and carry it himself, but I kept my temper. On the way, Jiro carefully kept pace with the older boy while I walked meekly behind them.

The Kai horses are well known all over Japan; they are not large, but powerful, and if their legs are a little clumsy, they are all the stronger for that. We stable-boys always rode bareback; saddles were for our betters, and if we used whips they were merely switches cut from some bush or tree.

The horses immediately sensed that we had come to rob them of their freedom. They were not easy to catch, but finally we managed to drive a few into a corner of the fenced-off land. I caught mine, an older mare that did not put up much of a fight. Matazo also captured his mount. Jiro's horse escaped, and he ran after it, cursing and wildly shaking the stick he had cut for a whip in the air.

Matazo laughed good-naturedly and, handing me the reins of his horse, he ran off to help the younger boy. I knew that Jiro was a poor rider, and as I watched I understood why: he was scared of horses. I almost felt the tenseness of his body in my own as I saw him reach for the mane instead of the forelock of the horse.

He should talk to it, I mumbled to myself as I fondled the muzzle of my own mount and felt its warm breath on my neck. Again Jiro's horse managed to break away. He held on to the mane but had to let go in the end.

I could see that Matazo had shouted something at Jiro, but I could not hear what he had said. I only sensed that he was angry. Jiro walked sullenly toward me, looking down as if he were searching for something he had lost in the grass.

"He wants you to help him," he muttered as he took the reins of the two horses out of my hands. I barely glanced at him for fear he could read in my face the joy I felt at his disgrace. I ran to help Matazo corner the runaway horse.

It was a gelding only four years old with a white star on its forehead, young but not a difficult horse to handle. Now it stood with four other horses, watching us suspiciously as we approached. The horse was breathing heavily; Jiro had managed to frighten it. I held out my hands to show that I had nothing in them while I explained that I would not harm it. One of the other horses broke away and galloped across the field. I could sense that the gelding was debating whether to follow. I stood still but kept making low comforting sounds, and the horse lowered its head and nipped at a clump of grass that had tempted it. As I came up to it quietly, I stroked its neck and could feel the muscles tense and then relax as I moved my hand towards its head, scratching and petting all the time. At last my hand felt its forelock; I held it lightly as Matazo came with the bridle. It had not been difficult at all. The gelding was a gentle animal with no malice in it.

"He is no good with the beasts." The older boy looked towards Jiro, who was standing as far away from our horses as the length of the reins would allow. I said nothing for fear that I would say too much. As we walked up to Jiro I kept my hand on the gelding's neck.

Matazo was holding our horses and I was just about to give the reins to Jiro when he brought down his stick as hard as he could on the soft muzzle of the unsuspecting horse. With a piercing whinny almost like a human scream, the gelding rose on its hind legs, tearing the reins out of my hand. At last I lost my patience and flew at Jiro. At my first blow he fell and I jumped on top of him. I hit him as hard as I could. Again and again I drove my fist into his face until I suddenly realized that he was crying and not defending himself at all.

Matazo had tied the reins of our horses to a bush and stood silently watching us while we fought. When I rose he ordered Jiro to go to the river and wash himself and then turning to me he said, "You should not have let go of the reins."

"I am sorry," I said. I thought it wise not to try to defend myself by pointing out that Jiro's attack had been as much of a surprise to me as it had been to the horse. Besides, he was right — one should always be prepared for the unexpected.

"We will have to be very careful now. We must not chase it. I don't want it to get its legs caught in the reins; if it stumbles it may break one." The boy looked at the gelding, which had galloped down to the bank of the river.

"We will let it rest for a moment, though I don't think it will forget that blow in a hurry. When it has calmed down a little we will take our horses down with us — their presence will help to quiet him."

Matazo had been brought up with horses and knew their ways. When we finally caught the gelding it was still shaking with fear. I vowed that I would spend some time with it when we got back to the stables, for an unearned blow can undo a horse as well as a man.

As Matazo mounted his horse he took the reins of the gelding in his hands as well. By the gate of the meadow stood Jiro.

"Open it!" the older boy ordered, looking sternly at Jiro, whose face showed traces of my fists.

"When we get back we will tell them that the horse threw you and that you prefer walking," he said as we rode through.

We were six boys and young men who shared a room next to the stables. The master of Lord Akiyama's horses had a small hut of his own, but he often had his meals with us. The room had only an earthen floor and on this was spread a straw mat large enough to cover most of it. The mat was well-worn and had seen long service in other places before ending with us. We also had a low table made from rough wood at which we ate. The seating arrangement round this table was as rigidly adhered to as in a lord's mansion. At the head of the table, farthest from the door and any possible draft, sat the master of the stables. Next to him, in order of age and importance, came the rest of us, ending with me at the foot of the table next to the door and, unfortunately, beyond the reach of the straw mat.

It was also my job — it went with the seat — to go to the cookhouse and fetch our food. I did not really mind that so much; it could sometimes have the advantage of some extra bit of food if the cook was in good humor. That evening Matazo ordered Jiro to fetch the food. For a moment Jiro and I looked at each other like young cocks ready to fight, then his face flushed and he turned away quickly and walked off to fetch our food. When he came back I saw traces of tears on his face; even then I could not feel sorry for him as I recalled the blow he had given the horse. That night I sat for the first time on the straw mat. The others acted as if they had not noticed the change. I felt it was their way of showing their approval.

{6}

A Night at Toko-ji Temple

Each year that passes is usually remembered by some particular incident that happened during it. A mighty ruler would probably recall the years by the battles he has won. For the poor, the year's weather was usually what it was best remembered by. That is not surprising, for when there is a drought it is the poor who starve, and if the river bursts its banks it is their houses that are swept away. Death, too, can often give its name to a year: "It was the year my mother died" or "that winter when we lost our youngest son." Life is not all tragedy. There are happy events too — years when the harvest is abundant and the river stays within its banks.

Shortly after my fight with Jiro, he was removed to the small castle at Akiyama. If my twelfth year could best be recalled by that "battle," and remembered with a grin, the event that marked my fourteenth would make no-one smile. It was fall when it happened, just as the last of the trees were losing their leaves. By that time I had moved up a bit on the mat and had reached a position among the others that was securely based upon my ability with the horses. We had also been given better clothing, for Lord Akiyama did not wish his servants to look like beggars. I was well satisfied with myself, knowing that I cut a fine figure when I rode through the town upon some errand for my master.

It was late in the day, just when the shadows grow large before they disappear into the night, that I heard someone shout "Taro!" I was standing by the corner of the stable and, in the dusk, I did not at first recognize who had called me, but I answered willingly enough. As I walked closer I realized that it was Lord Akiyama himself. I was surprised, for it was most unusual for him to come to the stables.

"Saddle two horses. I want you to accompany someone to Toko-ji. You are to wait for him there."

I was about to fulfill his command and had already taken a few steps in the direction of the stables when he called me back.

"One ought to have a few servants who have had their tongues cut out." Lord Akiyama grinned. "Since I have none that are mute, I hope at least to have a few who are clever enough not to speak of everything they see or hear."

I bowed deeply, in this way conveying the message that I hoped to be among such trusted servants. Lord Akiyama nodded as if to say, equally silently, "We shall see if that is true." Then he told me to bring the horses to the gate and to wait there.

Lord Akiyama had ordered me to saddle two horses. Though I preferred to ride bareback, I was pleased, for I was aware that it was an honor. The years had not lessened my desire to be numbered among the samurai and, to me, the saddle symbolized that rank and gave me renewed hope of attaining it.

I selected two horses that were fine animals but not showy. Somehow I felt that there was something secret and dark about the whole affair that did not call for horses that were too easily recognizable.

I had waited only a short while when Lord Akiyama came with a young samurai dressed very plainly. I recognized him immediately — he was Takeda Katsuyori, the son of Lord Shingen. I had seen him often enough, always splendidly dressed and usually riding one of his father's best horses. I guessed by the plainness of his dress and the fact that he had come to Lord Akiyama to borrow one of his horses that he did not wish to be recognized. Silently, I held the horse as he swung himself into the saddle, then I mounted my own horse. Lord Katsuyori leaned forward for a moment and said something to Lord Akiyama in so low a voice that I could not hear. Then he spurred his horse, and I followed him into the dusk.

Many strange things had taken place at Toko-ji. The temple is large, yet few go to worship there. It was in this temple that Suwa Yorishige had been prisoner, and there he had killed himself or had been murdered. Suwa Yorishige was Lord Katsuyori's grandfather. Lord Takeda had not only defeated Lord Suwa and taken his lands from him, but he had made his daughter his mistress; Katsuyori was her son. As we rode through the night, I pondered on all this and could not help wondering what the young man riding in front of me was thinking. Was he recalling his grandfather's death or his mother's disgrace, for should she not have killed herself rather than share Lord Takeda Shingen's bed? Lady Suwa was long dead; she had died when her son Katsuyori was nine years old. Was he loyal to her memory or to his mighty father?

The ride to Toko-ji temple would not have taken long in daylight, especially since we were riding fine horses. But the night soon grew so dark that we could not even let the horses trot. Once something in the gloom frightened Lord Katsuyori's horse and for a moment I thought he might be thrown, but he managed to bring the animal under control. When we came to the gate of the temple, Lord Katsuyori dismounted and, without a word, handed me the reins of his horse. I guessed that I was not to enter the temple grounds, but to wait for him hidden in the dark night outside.

Not one word had he spoken to me during the ride. Did he believe that I did not know who he was, or had he thought me not worthy of wasting his breath on? I sat down on a large stone near the temple gate. The night was cool; winter was not far away. In the distance a dog howled dismally as if it were in pain. I shivered, not so much from the cold as from fear. I wished Lord Katsuyori would come back so we could leave the dismal place.

The young lord did not return and the hours climbed by as slowly as if they were years. At last a tiny sickle moon rose over the mountains near the temple, setting off their black shadow against the star-filled night. Still Lord Katsuyori did not come. I waited patiently and as I sat and listened to the quiet breathing of the horses I was thankful for their company, for I feared that the place was filled with the ghosts of all the unhappy people who had died there. Suddenly I felt that something horrible was about to take place inside the temple walls, a premonition not so much of something evil but rather of something terribly sad happening in the darkness beyond. One of the horses whinnied softly and shook itself as if it too had sensed that all was not well in the still night. I put my hand up and stroked its neck to calm it; I thought it was important that I should not be noticed.

The tiny moon had set and I guessed that it would soon be the hour of the tiger when, suddenly, a young monk appeared. He did not greet me but merely stared while he stood so close that I could have touched him if I had held out my hand. I stared back. He had a mole near his nose and I thought, I shall remember you by that. As suddenly as he had come, he disappeared, after making a strange unpleasant grimace. Had he been sent by someone to spy, I wondered. Around my shoulders I wore a saddle-cloth that I had taken from the stable to keep me warm, and that had hidden my clothing, which had the crest of Lord Akiyama on it and was of his color.

Soon Lord Katsuyori came. As he took the reins I held out to him, his face was close to mine; it was white as I imagine a ghost's would be, and equally lifeless. He tarried a moment before mounting his horse and I wondered if he was going to speak to me. Then he rode away at a sharp trot in the darkness and I followed, holding the reins tight for fear my horse would stumble. As we returned to Kofuchu the stars were growing faint. Soon the night would be over. Near Tsutsujigasaki Castle, Lord

Katsuyori dismounted and handed me his reins as silently as he had done at Toko-ji temple. He made a slight movement with his right hand, which I took as a sign of my dismissal. I was tired and cold as I returned to the stables. I lingered there for a moment, because it was warm and the smell of the beasts was pleasant. Something had happened at Toko-ji, something important: I did not know quite what it was, or — maybe that was not true — maybe I knew. As I lay down in my place in our room and wrapped my blanket around me, again I saw Lord Katsuyori's face in front of me with its ashen pallor.

If you are six sleeping in one room, then you are awakened when the others get up, regardless of the fact that you went to bed just before sunrise. Even though I turned toward the wall and hid my face, I soon had to give up trying to get any more rest. I had already made up my mind what story to tell if any of my friends should ask what errand I had been on. It would not do to act the mute, for that would only make everyone all the more curious. Still, I am not sure the others were satisfied that my tale was true, but I was spared further questioning when the youngster who had been sent to the kitchen returned not only with our breakfast porridge but with such important news that my whereabouts the night before was forgotten.

"Yoshinobu-sama has killed himself!" The youngster's eyes were shining with excitement. "It is true! He killed himself at Toko-ji temple. He committed seppuku this morning. The cook heard it from a samurai!"

The youngster was enjoying being the center of attention. Such news as that Lord Shingen's son had committed hara-kiri was so unusual a breakfast conversation that the porridge was allowed to grow cold. Everyone had something to say, some comment to make, and everyone felt sorry for Yoshinobu. It was hard punishment for his revolt; after all, his father had done the same when he was young. Lord Takeda Shingen had been only twenty-one years old when he had led an insurrection against his father, Takeda Nobutora, and sent him into exile in Suruga. The old man was still alive, and they say he dreamed of vengeance against his son. I listened to the babble around me but said nothing. The keeper of Lord Akiyama's stables, a man older than the rest of us, asked, "Does anyone know who was his kaishaku-nin?"

Everyone looked at one another and no-one answered for no-one knew.

The porridge was bolted quickly, for all were eager to get out and about. Servants are ever ready to gossip about their master's household. The news of the day was like some precious gift bestowed among them, and they were eager to discuss it with others, longing for new ears to pour their opinions into. Soon I was left alone to contemplate what had happened during the night and the unanswered question. Who had been the kaishaku-nin when Yoshinobu had committed seppuku?

The kaishaku-nin's part in that ceremony is not one to be envied. When a man who is committing hara-kiri has entered his dirk in his belly and drawn it across, cutting his stomach open, it is the kaishaku-nin's work to finish his life as quickly as possible, to cut short the pain by severing the head from the body. For a moment I had thought that Katsuyori had been his brother's kaishaku-nin. But the longer I thought about it, the more I realized that he could not have been. For the kaishaku-nin is always a friend of the man who commits seppuku, not his rival; besides, he is usually older, and Katsuyori was much younger than his half-brother Yoshinobu.

Suddenly it occurred to me that there might not have been any need for a kaishaku-nin. That something worse and more disgraceful had taken place in Toko-ji than I had imagined. Had Yoshinobu been executed by his father's command, and had it been Katsuyori's duty to take that warrant of death to the temple?

{7}

Zazen

In the spring of the year following Yoshinobu's death at Toko-ji temple, I left Kofuchu for Iida Castle in Ina district where my master Lord Akiyama ruled. Something had happened that made me only too pleased to leave Kofuchu for a while. It was a foolish thing, the root of which was in my pride.

The priest who had been a friend of Togan had been kind to me, and when I asked him to teach me to write he had willingly done so. At first my letters were badly drawn and I handled my brush clumsily; to write well you must hold the brush firmly yet lightly. If you grab it as a man drowning grasps a piece of wood floating by, you will make many splotches and stain your paper rather than write on it. On the other hand, if you handle your brush as gingerly as you would a snake filled with poison, you will fare no better. Yet by that winter I had learned to write fairly well and knew enough characters to be able to compose a letter. In my station as a stable-boy there was no need for writing, a fact of which some of the other boys left me in little doubt. But there is a pleasure in the task, and I could sometimes spend hours writing the most complicated characters that I knew with a pointed stick in the dust.

Most samurai know how to write and this, rather than

a thirst for knowledge, had been my reason for learning. Had I been satisfied with this, I should not have gotten into trouble, for the priest I learned from was a kind man who humbly served Buddha and searched for the Way. But as I learned to read and could, with great difficulty, make my way through the text of the sutras, I began to be dissatisfied with my humble teacher.

Most, but not all, of the samurai practice Zen. There are many sects of Buddhism, and if there is one road that is particularly well-trodden by those who wear silk, it is Zen. Not only had I never forgotten my ancestry, I had, in truth, made it a lot loftier than it had been. After his death, my father advanced remarkably among the retainers of Lord Uesugi Kenshin until from an ordinary samurai he had become Lord Uesugi's chief general. Zen attracted me not so much as the Way of Enlightenment, but because of the companions I might encounter on that road.

At En-ko temple, not far from Lord Akiyama's place, Zazen was held in the early mornings. I asked one of the monks for permission to attend and it was granted. I had carefully washed myself and was wearing a blue linen kimono and new straw sandals when I presented myself at the temple just as the hour of the hare was over. A young monk looked at me carefully; he bowed, but not humbly as he saw that my kimono was threadbare linen, not cotton or silk. He showed me the way to a Zazen hall on the right side of the main temple. There were others there already, seated facing the wall. I bowed, casting a quick glance at their clothes to judge who my fellow travelers were. The monk indicated my place and I sat down, first taking a good look at my neighbors to the right and to the left, which earned me an admonition from the monk. I was furious, for it was obvious to me that I was seated among people of no greater importance than myself. There must have been two halls: one where the samurai did Zazen, the other for the likes of me. Slowly a little sense crept into my head; it would not have been wise of the monks to seat a samurai next to someone of no importance. The food of a monk is but a sparse meal, but even those meager ingredients must come from somewhere. To offend those who wear the sword would be foolish; only those who are truly devout in their worship of Lord Buddha have a weapon as strong as the iron blade.

When you are practicing Zazen you sit immobile, as if you were a statue of Buddha. You must attempt to empty your mind of all thoughts, of all the vanities of this world. I do not know if it can be done, for I have never succeeded. Perhaps others did; many claimed so. Just as many a samurai will claim that he does not know fear, though he can easily recall what the cold fear of death felt like, so many Buddhist priests will claim a holiness that they do not possess. Pride can take refuge in rags and humbleness as well as in silken robes.

While you are doing Zazen, a monk walks with silent steps round the hall. He carries a long wooden stick called a kyosaku, which he holds in his hands with the same reverence that a samurai handles an unsheathed sword. He uses the kyosaku to give you a smart crack on the shoulders. This is supposed to keep your mind from wandering, but it never did mine. Sometimes when I knew that the monk had just passed me, I would have a quick look around to see if any of the others were as restless as I was. With shame, I must admit that I never caught any of them doing the same. They were all sitting as still as a row of stone Buddhas. Then I would return my gaze to the floor in front of me, feeling ashamed.

Until the blossoms of the peach trees had fallen, I practiced Zazen twice a week. Not only did I have to get up earlier on such days, but I missed my breakfast porridge. This was more of a hardship than it sounds, for we were always hungry at the best of times and one meal missed did not mean that you received a greater share of the next.

It was usually the same young monk who was the jikido, the holder of the wooden stick. As I was always stealing glances around me, I knew him well, not by his face, for I would not have dared look up. No, I knew him by his feet. I could always manage to catch a glimpse of them as he walked by; he had the peculiarity of having eight long dark hairs on the big toe of his right foot and nine on the same toe of his left. I counted them during one session — this was not so difficult, for the jikido walks very slowly round the hall, moving his feet almost as if he were in a trance. I was a little shocked when I noticed one day that the jikido's feet were hairless. Forgetting myself, I turned and looked at the monk as he came near me. At the sight of his face I almost cried aloud in both surprise and alarm. The monk stopped and looked at me, he bowed, and then lifting the kyosaku he brought it down with as much force as he could muster. A loud crack was heard and for a moment I feared he had done my shoulder an injury, but I managed to smile and bow as if I had felt nothing. The monk also bowed and for a moment he too smiled, but his smile was a grimace like the one that had disfigured his face that night at Toko-ji temple.

After Zazen was over there was a service with reading of sutras. I had always liked to chant the prayers to Buddha with the others, but that day I decided to leave as soon as Zazen had ended. Once outside where no-one could see me, I rubbed my shoulder. It was still smarting from the blow. I was in no doubt that the monk had hit me so hard out of spite; having seen me with Katsuyori he had assumed that I was one of his servants. The monk was obviously one who had sided with Yoshinobu, or at least, he had no liking for Katsuyori and that was why he had struck me.

At the temple gate I was stopped by two samurai. I had never seen them before and guessed them to be a couple of ronins, wandering samurai whose swords were for sale.

One of them grabbed me by the shoulder and, turning to his friend, asked, "Was it not him?"

The other pretended to look me over carefully, screwing up his face as if he were in great doubt. Finally he turned to his comrade, saying, "I think it was he who stole my purse."

"I have never seen you before!" I shouted angrily.

"He says he has never seen you before." The samurai who held me repeated my words dolefully.

"Is that not what they all say?" The samurai shook his head.

Out of the corner of my eye I caught sight of the young monk — he was standing not far away, watching us. This is all of your making, I thought. Then realizing that I was in great danger, my anger left me, and turning to the samurai I said, "You must be mistaken."

"He says you're mistaken." The samurai who had decided to be my echo smiled like a cat who has cornered a mouse.

"I remember quite clearly that the fellow had a nose and two ears." The samurai made as if to check that I was similarly equipped. "If we cut off one of them, we would always be able to recognize him again. . . ."

"I do not think my master would like that." I tried to keep all fear out of my voice.

"He says his master wouldn't like it." The samurai relaxed his hold on my shoulder a little. "I wonder who his master is?"

"I think if you shouted Shiro, he might answer to it." The samurai who had accused me of stealing his purse laughed. Katsuyori had been called Shiro as a boy; the gibe was an insult, but if I were really Katsuyori's servant this was a foolish and dangerous game. There and then I decided that they should not learn from my mouth who my master was. I was wearing a thin summer kimono that could have belonged to anyone whose purse had never contained gold.

"It was he! He was there that night, I remember him." The young monk had slipped up unnoticed; his interference seemed to annoy the two samurai. As there was no longer any point in accusing me of being a thief, the older of the two samurai changed his tactics.

"The sleeves of a poor man blow lightly in a breeze." The samurai grinned at me and I noticed that his front teeth were missing.

"Sometimes what the eyes have seen or the ears heard can be worth something to put in one's sleeve . . ."

"A good servant sees nothing and hears even less," I countered, giving a slight bow to show my humility.

"That is true, but there are few of them." The samurai put on a grave air of approval, which made him look even more of a scoundrel. "Sometimes even the best of servants may remember where they were on a certain night, who they were with, and what happened." Suddenly the samurai changed his tone and whispered, "For if they don't remember they may lose an ear. . . ."

I had spied some samurai coming toward us; they had been to Zazen and were now on the way back to their homes. As they reached the gate, I took a step backward, bowed to the two samurai, and the one who held me by the shoulder let go as the others approached.

"I shall remember everything you said, master," I said in a loud voice, then I turned and ran. As I had expected, the two men did not want to lose their dignity by chasing me in front of the other samurai.

I ran all the way to Lord Akiyama's mansion. Only

when I was inside its gates did I feel safe. Sooner or later I would be sent on some errand, for we stable-boys were also messengers, and then . . .

Lord Akiyama was the governor of Iida Castle so he was seldom in Kofuchu, but I felt that I had to tell him what had happened. I presented myself at the big house after the evening meal and asked to see Akiyama Nobutora, my master's father. I had to wait until he had finished his meal, and finally I was led into his room. I fell on my knees and bowed until my forehead touched the mat on which I was kneeling.

"Who are you and what do you want? It is not a seemly time to disturb someone." The voice was powerful and had none of the trembling quality that so often disfigures the speech of the old.

I looked up but remained in my kneeling position. The old samurai had just finished his meal; the little table was still in front of him. I had seen him before but never so close. Though neither tall nor powerfully built, he was an imposing man. His face was tanned the color of old leather; his eyes were large, but he kept them half-closed, giving his face an expression of cunning. In as few words as possible I told him who I was and why I had come.

When I had finished, Lord Nobutora scrutinized me silently, then he nodded as if he were agreeing with some thought that had just occurred to him. Finally he spoke.

"Tomorrow morning before the cock crows, get on your way to Iida Castle to my son; you will be given a letter from me. . . . Do not take one of the best horses, nor one who may go lame. . . . Don't saddle it; it is best for youngsters like you to ride without."

For a moment the old man smiled, and I thought, He can recall his own youth and the many days he spent on horseback then. He made a motion with his right hand as if to shoo away a fly. I understood and, bowing deeply once more, I rose and walked backward from his presence.

8

On the Road

The letter that I was to deliver to Lord Akiyama was given to me before nightfall, with four copper coins. I went to the stable to choose a horse and decided upon a mare, a gentle animal I had grown fond of. I hardly slept that night, since this was to be my first long journey. As soon as the first pale light appeared in the sky I was up and about. There was little to pack. I owned two pairs of straw sandals, one worn and one almost new, the threadbare summer kimono, and a few other clothes. I made a bundle of these things and folded up my bedding and put it away. Careful not to disturb my still sleeping roommates, I slipped out of the room.

There was a promise of a beautiful day in the pale blue sky where a few stars were still visible. Before mounting my horse I paused and looked around. I wanted later to be able to recall what everything had looked like. The mountains behind Tsutsujigasaki Castle were still clouded in an early morning mist. Since I had learned to write, I sometimes wrote poetry. This, too, was merely trying to imitate my betters, as several of the lords prided themselves on their abilities, and even the great Lord Takeda Shingen had been an accomplished poet in his youth. Now I composed one verse.

Shyly clad in the morning mist,
The mountains retreat into the sky.

I was pleased with my accomplishment and with myself as I rode through the sleeping town westward toward Shinano and Iida Castle.

It was just in the beginning of the fifth month; greenery was sprouting everywhere and in the valley the newly planted rice stood like little soldiers in long orderly rows in the paddies. By the time the sun rose above the mountains in the east I had left the town behind me. Midmorning I stopped by a small shrine surrounded by tall pine trees whose shade invited a traveler to pause on a sunny day. The caretaker of the shrine was an elderly man who lived in a small house nearby. It was a Hachiman shrine, a god that Takeda Shingen favored above the other Shinto gods. The caretaker invited me into his house and served me a cup of tea. He was eager to hear news from Kofuchu and plied me with questions. Several times he would touch upon the death of Yoshinobu and hint that he thought it a great pity that he should have died so young. The old man pointed out that Yoshinobu's mother came of an exalted line, and her father had been one of the most important aristocrats in Kyoto.

"Did you realize," he almost shouted, "that that noble family is related to the Heavenly Descended?" The keeper of the shrine became so excited that he struck the palm of one hand against the other for emphasis. I mumbled my agreement with a bored air, for I was not going to let him realize that I had not known of Lady Sanjo's relationship to the Emperor.

From Lady Sanjo he passed on to Katsuyori's mother. Just as much as he held the one in awe, he held the other in contempt.

"What was Lady Suwa but a kept woman? Nothing more!" he declared. Agreeing whole-heartedly with her husband, his wife chimed in with even more vindictiveness. I had long ceased nodding and had given up the appearance of listening in the hope that this would make the old lady cease her spitefulness. She was as difficult to stop as a newly erupting volcano; there was nothing else to be done but to flee. I rose hastily and, bowing, thanked them for the tea. The old lady smiled sourly, showing her toothless gums.

Once seated on the back of my mare, I could not help but think of the sad fate of Lady Suwa. Takeda Shingen had defeated and killed her father and then had made her his mistress. She had been friendless in the castle, for had not all the women and servants been too aware that she was related to no emperor? Totally defenseless, alone among strangers, she had died when her son Katsuyori was nine years old. Some said that Takeda Shingen had loved her, but more certain it was that his wife, Lady Sanjo, had hated her.

Some men were driving a flock of oxen. I held my horse and watched them. As they passed, the men bowed and my face flushed with pleasure; I felt sure they had taken me for a samurai's son. At noon I rested by a river. I ate the two rice-balls I had been given, but I was still hungry. I counted my coins as if I were expecting them to have multiplied in my sleeve. There were still only four. They would buy me a night's lodging and an evening meal. Since it was spring and there was grass enough I would need nothing for my mare. Two monks came by, removing their straw sandals before wading across the river; they eyed me for a moment to decide if I were worth begging from. They had traveled far; their heads were unshaven as if it were long since they had rested in a temple. The older one nodded to me and I returned the greeting without enthusiasm, for I did not care much for beggar monks. The habit of a monk is easy to obtain and will often hide a robber in disguise or a bandit fleeing to save his life.

In a small village in the borderland between Kai and Shinano I found an inn where I could have shelter and an evening meal for three of my four coins. The innkeeper was big and fat and so lazy that he sat at the entrance to his establishment like a wayside Buddha. He had a whole flock of female attendants who eagerly performed all tasks at their master's command. Their roundness gave hope of a good meal, and I was not disappointed. A fresh fish was the main attraction. There were mushrooms and leeks and rice cooked with beans, prepared not in my honor but because it was the seventh anniversary of the death of the innkeeper's father. I was given sake; the innkeeper kept me company and plied me with questions as well as with rice wine. The sake was of his own making, he told me, and there was none in all of Kai that could touch it for strength and purity. The innkeeper was not a modest man; he knew his own worth and was proud of it. He claimed to be of samurai descent and declared that his grandfather had had so many sons that if you had divided his swords among them all, they would each have received but a knife for peeling apples. Later in the evening friends arrived. The room we were sitting in was the same one in which I was going to sleep, so there was no point in calling for my bedding. The innkeeper had managed to pry from me that I was in the service of Lord Akiyama and that I was heading for Iida Castle. He took for granted that I was a messenger and I did not trouble to inform him of my lowly position as a stable-boy. Those who were messengers to Lord Shingen — *tsukai ban shu* they were called — were all sons of important lords and samurai.

As the rice wine loosened tongues, matters of deep and serious substance were discussed. An old man, with such deep furrows in his face that I thought it must have taken eighty winters to draw them, upheld the power of the Emperor and declared that before the first Shogun, when the Emperor had ruled supreme, all had been well in Japan. The innkeeper would not agree with this; what was wrong with the present, he held, was that we had no ruler worthy of the name.

"Yoshiaki is not a bull but a calf! He is no ruler — he was made Shogun by Oda Nobunaga. . . . Better it would have been if Oda himself had taken the reins." Suddenly the innkeeper became aware of my presence and added hurriedly, "But best of all would be if a Takeda ruled

Japan. . . . If Takeda Shingen were Shogun then peace would come to all."

I smiled, accepting the flattery for what it was worth, and wondered if there were many followers of Oda Nobunaga here.

"There are many great lords, and all of them would like to rule. Would not . . ." I hesitated before mentioning the lord my father had served — "would not Uesugi Kenshin also make a good ruler?"

One of the women had brought in a big dish of pickles. The innkeeper carefully selected one, popped it into his mouth, and then shook his head.

"He thinks only of fighting; he is a hawk in the sky, but Shingen is an eagle. To fight — bah! That is nothing! You must know when and why you fight and then you will win. . . . Soon the war will come — the eagles are gathering. Takeda Shingen is an eagle and Oda Nobunaga too, but Kenshin" — the innkeeper grinned, showing his teeth — "he is only a samurai, a two-sword man."

I thought to myself, And you, you are a lord. I felt certain that each night when the innkeeper retired to sleep and closed his eyes, he was transformed into one of the great lords of Japan and ruled the country until daybreak made him again a poor innkeeper in a small and unimportant village.

"Now if only the Emperor . . ." the old man began, but he got no chance to finish for at that moment the innkeeper's brother arrived. Taking advantage of the new arrival, the innkeeper suggested I might want to sleep and that they would all retire to the kitchen. I had no wish to continue the discussion, though it was quite plain that I was not invited to partake further in the party. Bowing politely to them all, I excused myself and went outside to see how my mare was. She was grazing peacefully in a small fenced field; below the inn was a flooded paddy field, the moon had come out and was reflected in the water. Not a breath of air moved; in the stillness I tried to compose a verse.

Inside the mirror of the ricefield
The moon hides, yet the wanderer found it.

The last part did not satisfy me and I returned to my room. I was lucky to be the only guest; I had feared the company of ronins, masterless samurai little better than robbers. As I lay down I reflected that the innkeeper had been right in one thing at least: soon a great battle would take place to decide who was to rule Japan. If, I thought as my eyes closed, Takeda Shingen became Shogun and master of the whole country, then Lord Akiyama might become . . . And then I fell asleep and dreamed of my master's and my own greatness.

{9}

Iida Castle

"Yoshinobu was in too much of a hurry. He ran on his way to power, and if you run, it is easy to stumble and fall." Lord Akiyama finished reading the letter I had brought from his father.

"Man's life is short. Rushing through it does not make it longer." Lord Akiyama shook his head. "I was sorry for Yoshinobu, yet he had to die. Disloyalty is like a sickness, it spreads. The foolish youth had succeeded in dividing his father's retainers. I felt sorry, too, for Lord Shingen. It must have been a terrible decision to make. Yet he had no choice, and what you told my father proves that there are still some among us who cannot be trusted." Lord Akiyama, who had looked so stern, suddenly smiled as he glanced down at me.

"You have grown. Soon you will have outgrown your name; I must find a new one for you."

I flushed and bowed but did not dare to speak for fear my voice would tremble and become a child's.

"Did you know who those two samurai were, whom they belonged to?"

"They were ronins, my lord, I am certain. They spoke as if they came from far away." I hesitated a moment and then added, "They were poor, too."

"That you may be sure of, for it was the discontented

who sided with the young fool, those who thought to climb by the disgrace of others." Lord Akiyama grinned. "Those who wear silk seldom revolt, for they do not know the bitterness of a night wind, nor the language of a hungry stomach. You must stay here for a while. You can be one of my messengers. . . . That is, unless the air of the stable suits you so well that you would prefer to stay there?"

"My lord, I would serve you in whatever post you may decide." I bowed so low that my forehead nearly touched the mat on which I was kneeling.

"Well then, you shall be a messenger, for I think you have outgrown being a page."

I could not help smiling and, for the first time, it occurred to me that Lord Akiyama had no children of his own. His wife had been childless and had died some years ago; although his brothers had children, he acknowledged none of his nephews as his heir. He had given me the name Taro, a name usually given to a first-born child. Could he have thought of adopting me? Lord Akiyama was playing with his fan, opening and shutting it with quick little movements, and now he held it up and indicated that I could leave. I bowed once more, so deeply this time that my forehead indeed touched the mat, then I rose and walked backward out of the room.

Lord Akiyama's messengers were all young soldiers, sons of his captains. I was the youngest among them, and again I had to be as humble as my youth demanded. But I did not mind, for well I knew how much this new position had advanced me: no longer was it a foolish fancy to dream that I would become a samurai. We messengers were a superior kind of servant who carried orders given by our betters. We were but six; the other five had been pages and brought up in court life. The oldest among us had served as a page at Tsutsujigasaki Castle. According to him Iida Castle was but a poor man's hut compared with the Takeda mansion, and he had the deepest contempt for the fashions and habits of our "court."

The district Lord Akiyama ruled over was vast. Samurai retainers and vassals who were lords of villages or mountain valleys would often arrive to consult Lord Akiyama, to pay him taxes, or to ask him to arbitrate in some dispute. It was our duty to greet such visitors and to escort them to the room Lord Akiyama used to receive them. I quickly learned that our position had a lucrative side; a little sleeve money could be easily earned — one need only pretend that Lord Akiyama was busy that day to earn a few coppers. The oldest messengers especially were expert at this game and played it to perfection. It was only the poor or middling wealthy farmers whom we could pluck; a samurai would know better than to put coins in our sleeves and we than to make any attempt to ask him. Sometimes a gift was freely bestowed on us, but then it was after the samurai had been received by Lord Akiyama and more to celebrate that the result of the meeting had been favorable.

The first time I was offered a few copper coins by a timid old man, I indignantly refused them. He thought he had not offered me enough and immediately doubled the amount. I forced the money back on him, and from his tattered kimono he drew a purse as slender as he was to show that he could give me no more. When he finally understood that I did not ask for money and would guide him to Lord Akiyama without a fee, he embarrassed me by bowing and scraping in front of me even though he was old enough to be my grandfather.

The scene had been observed by two of the other messengers, one of whom took me severely to task, hinting that my time as a messenger might be short if I were to repeat such behavior. I mumbled something about not being a beggar monk, which resulted in his being doubly insulted and accusing me of calling him a beggar. He reminded me that I was but a boy still and then touched upon my former home, the stable. I kept my temper, only muttering in my defense that the man had looked so poor. This made the young soldier laugh, and he pointed out that the slenderer the purse, the easier it was to open. I kept my gaze away for fear that he would read the contempt on my face and stared instead at the floor. When he had admonished me and walked away, I felt a childish urge to spit upon the floor where he had stood, but the other young man still stood there watching me, a smile upon his face.

"Are you one of those Buddhist sages who grows fat on wisdom and clothes himself in holiness?" he asked, and before I had a chance to reply, he continued, "If so, then Iida Castle is not the right place for you. You should search out some temple or hut in the mountains where the vanities of the world could not tempt you."

I shook my head in anger, feeling I had been unjustly

treated. The young man went on to explain a little about our position as messengers. It seemed that we were never paid yet were expected not to dress in rags. Lord Akiyama well knew how we managed to obtain the little money we had; great demands were made upon his purse, so he was only too glad to close his eyes to our affairs. I, who was badly in need of clothing, finally understood that I had been foolish in refusing the coins, but I could not help but mention once more the poverty of the farmer who had had no more in his purse than what he had offered me. The young man, Yoshitoki, put his hand on my shoulder.

"Charity should always be mute," he said, "for those who never practice it find that virtue an affront. Remember to do your good deeds as secretly as if they were crimes." Laughing good-naturedly, he added, "But they say you are Lord Akiyama's pet, and he would not dislike you for what you have done."

Everyone needs a friend, and soon I was telling Yoshitoki the story of my life, how I had been presented as a gift by the great Lord Takeda Shingen to Lord Akiyama after my parents had been killed. He laughed when I told him how I had defended myself with the bamboo sword against the soldier who had been ordered to kill me. My tale was a good one, he declared, and augured well for my future, for even the great Lord Takeda Shingen would not forget me. He was unfortunate, he confessed, for his father had gone to his grave unnoticed and had left so little property behind that Yoshitoki's older brother had had to marry a girl whose father had never held more than a hoe in his hand. It worried him that he might have the same fate, or perhaps a worse. He had three sisters, one of whom he offered me in marriage, saying that he felt sure she would make an excellent wife. I declined the honor, as I felt that I was neither in age nor in property ready for such a venture. Yoshitoki laughed and declared that I had plenty of time to think about the proposal as his oldest sister was only eight.

Such was the beginning of my friendship with Yoshitoki, a youngster who looked wide-eyed at the world and found much in it worthy of his laughter. Soon he knew all my secrets, my small vanities as well as my hopes and ambitions. Yoshitoki himself had few of either; he was satisfied in being a friend to others rather than demanding friendship for himself. Even now the name Yoshitoki carries the soft warmth of the spring breeze to me.

{10}

Yoshitoki

My fifteenth summer was as free of troubles as the spring sky is of clouds. Two weeks after my arrival in Iida Castle a messenger came from Kofuchu bearing a dispatch from Lord Takeda. The messenger was not one of the usual young soldiers but a high-ranking samurai who had traveled with ten mounted retainers. He was alone with Lord Akiyama for several hours; we never found out what they had discussed, for the doors and screens were kept firmly closed. The next day Lord Akiyama announced that he would leave for Tsutsujigasaki Castle in a few days' time, taking most of the soldiers and samurai with him.

Only a small garrison was to be left at Iida Castle under the command of an old samurai whom we youngsters had dubbed "Lord Inago" because of the way he walked. One of his legs was stiff from an old wound, which gave him a jumping gait like a grasshopper's. For two days I was kept in suspense, not knowing if I was to go or to stay at the castle. When I finally learned that the youngest among the messengers were to remain, I was bitterly disappointed. Fate had cheated me of an opportunity to show my worth on the battlefield.

Lord Akiyama left at the head of his army on a beautiful day; the sun shone from a clear sky and made armor and banners appear doubly bright and colorful. By this time we all knew that Lord Takeda was planning to invade the province of Suruga as soon as the rice harvest was over. As I watched some of the older messengers ride by, I felt so angry that I was near to tears. Suddenly I felt a hand on my shoulder, and I looked around and saw Yoshitoki.

"Some of them will come back heroes," he said, "but there are others who will not come back at all. The heroes will be given land and some of the spoil of battle by Lord Takeda. The others, those who won't come back," Yoshitoki lowered his voice to a whisper, "they will be given land, too, but not so much — just enough for a grave."

Naturally I knew that people died in battle, that the ground was sometimes covered in corpses after the fighting had ceased. Although I had heard of rivers that turned red with the blood of the dying, I had never imagined myself among them. I nodded soberly as if those very words he had spoken expressed my feelings too. Yoshitoki smiled; I am sure that he knew what I had been thinking.

"We are lucky," he said. "We shall have the castle almost to ourselves. The Grasshopper is easy-going and will not need us much; we will be free to hunt and fish. . . . I am now the oldest of the messengers."

All of a sudden I realized that the two messengers whom I liked least were to accompany Lord Akiyama. It was true what Yoshitoki had said: we would be free to hunt and fish. Lord Inago would not be a hard master, that was certain. As the last of the soldiers passed by, I turned to Yoshitoki.

"I was angry because I was left behind," I confessed. "I wanted to be among the soldiers whom Lord Akiyama took along. I was very foolish."

"No!" Yoshitoki shook his head. "I think you are destined to live and I to die. That is why you are eager to prove yourself in battle and I am pleased to have yet another year to live." He grinned and stretched himself.

For several months Yoshitoki and I explored every path and valley within a day's ride of the castle. We tracked the deer and the wild boar and surprised a wolf in her lair. Armed with bows and arrows, we killed many a rabbit and brought back enough game to please Lord Inago and make him only too willing to let us hunt for more. We were up so early that we often saw the fox returning from the nightly hunt; we rose with the sun and, tired as a couple of bear cubs that have played all day, we fell asleep as it set.

Yet while we strutted the earth like immortals, the warmth of the friendship between Yoshitoki and me was so intense that the memory of it can even now warm the body of a frail old man. We were like two small clouds drifting in an endless sky.

Few duties kept us away from our pleasures, but at the end of the tenth month we were given an assignment. We were to carry a message to Kofuchu, to Tsutsujigasaki Castle. The best of the horses had gone with Lord Akiyama, but we were allowed to take our pick of the remainder. I was immensely pleased when we were given weapons, only a sword each, and again not of the best quality, but the same as the foot soldiers carried. We were also given a purse for the expenses during the journey and papers to prove that we were traveling on an errand for Lord Takeda, so that we did not have to pay toll at the gates on the road. We felt immensely important the morning we started out. Yoshitoki's horse was saddled, but I rode bareback as there was no saddle left in a condition to be used.

The first day passed uneventfully. We followed the road that runs along the bottom of the valley near the river; this is a well-traveled road with plenty of inns in the villages where food may be obtained. We felt very grand as we sat eating our meals and, like young lords, ordered the servant girl to bring more tea or another dish of rice.

On the second day we reached Takato Castle; here, too, the garrison was small and consisted of the very young and very oldest soldiers. They told us that Lord Shingen had been victorious and that the army was expected to return within a month. Lord Katsuyori, the governor of the castle, was not there but was with his father. As at Iida, an old and trusted samurai had been left in charge.

The following morning, just as we were leaving, two Buddhist monks appeared and asked permission to travel in our company. They were on foot but had an old horse carrying sutras that they were taking to a monastery in Kai. Though not pleased, we were flattered and tried to make excuses; the monks insisted that they would like our company for safety as we traveled through the mountains. They claimed to be followers of the sect of Nichiren traveling to the main temple of their sect, Kuon-ji. It is a sect of Buddhism I do not care much for; its adherents are strong-willed and quarrelsome. What is pleasant and agreeable in this world they regard as sinful; they are quick to attack others for their vanity, but I have always found them the vainest themselves. In his book of advice, the great general, Lord Kansuke, warns against quarrelsome traveling companions, but there was no getting rid of them so we set out just after sunrise.

The monks walked quickly and had little trouble keeping up with us; their bodies were thin and muscular, as if they were used to traveling. They were well past their youth, though still in the prime of their strength, and I could not help feeling that it was not long since their heads had been shaven for the first time. I felt sure that they had been sumarai, guessing this from the look of contempt the younger of them had given my sword, as if he had been used to better. They say that the blade of the sword is a mirror that reflects its owner's soul; if that is true, then mine was a sorry one.

Midmorning we rested by a small brook, first drinking from its clear water ourselves and then letting our horses quench their thirst. The two monks asked a lot of questions but answered few themselves. It struck me that there was not much point in carrying sutras to Kuon-ji; surely there were plenty of prayer rolls there already as the monks in the temple made them? I did not ask, for I suspected that our traveling companions were not monks but bandits. It was not so much our swords that they needed for protection, but our traveling permits. As couriers carrying a message from one castle to another we would be allowed through the toll-gates without much scrutiny and so would our traveling companions — our very presence would vouch for them. I glanced at Yoshitoki. The wary expression on his face convinced me that he had come to the same conclusion.

Just before noon we came to a path that led off to the right. We were now far into the mountains and one of the monks claimed that this was a short cut which would save us half a day's journey. The path was less traveled than the one we were on and looked best suited for some dark deed. I felt certain that should we enter it we would not return but would be left somewhere in the forest as food for foxes or wolves. I tried to ride ahead but the monks blocked the passage with their horse. My hand felt for the hilt of my sword, but before I had a chance to draw it our traveling companions drew two shiny and sharp-looking weapons from the pack on their horse.

"Young legs are best trained and grow strongest by walking!" said one of the monks with a grin while with his sword he indicated that we should dismount. I looked at Yoshitoki; he had drawn his sword and his horse was standing near the rump of the monks' nag. One of the monks was holding the reins, and the other was leaning against the flank of the animal. Suddenly Yoshitoki stuck his sword as hard as he could into the rump of their old nag. Whinnying loudly the horse jumped in pain, dragging one monk with her and throwing the other off balance. The road was free, so we dug our heels into the sides of our animals and galloped ahead.

We galloped until we thought ourselves safe, then reined in our horses and looked at each other.

"They were bandits!" we both exclaimed at the same moment and then started to laugh. This was high adventure, a story to tell on our return. Then I recalled that Lord Kansuke had also recommended that people who wanted to take short cuts should not be trusted. I told Yoshitoki this and he laughed, saying that the path we had not taken would surely have been a short cut to death.

There is nothing that can make a man feel more alive than to have been near death. Suddenly you realize what a precious gift your life is, and your eyes open to the beauty of the world around you. Such were our feelings as we traveled on. Once in a while we would glance at each other and then smile contentedly.

At sunset we reached the summit of the pass which led to Kai and Kofuchu. A few spear lengths from the road was a simple hut, and from it emerged a strange old creature, his hair white and unkempt and his kimono incredibly dirty.

"Please enter my humble home!" he said as he bowed. I glanced at Yoshitoki. The night was cold in the mountains. We dismounted, tied our horses to a tree, and followed the old man into his hut.

{11}

In the House of a Ghost

The hut was small and the door so low that even I had to bow my head to enter. In the center of the room stood a small iron grate where a charcoal fire smoldered, and on a tripod above it was an iron kettle from which a little stream of steam escaped, promising tea. The hut was cluttered with all sorts of worthless possessions. In one corner was a bundle of rags that I guessed was the owner's bedding.

We shall catch fleas or worse, I thought as I knelt down beside the charcoal brazier to warm my hands.

"From the top of the mountain all roads lead in only one direction — down." Our host was preparing tea; he moved in little abrupt movements, like a monkey, I thought.

"And from the bottom of the valley, the way can only be upward," I countered, wanting to show that I had understood what he referred to.

"The way of a holy man seeking the truth and the way of a samurai are not the same." The little man handed us teacups; strangely they were not chipped and were valuable, I thought.

"It is best when the vessel and what it contains are both of the same quality. We are not samurai, merely messengers for Lord Akiyama on our way to Kofuchu." I drank the tea; it had the perfect amount of bitterness to refresh you and was warm rather than hot.

"You live by yourself, grandfather," Yoshitoki stated rather than asked, and then added, "Do you not find it lonely?"

The ancient man laughed. To my surprise he had a full set of teeth.

"I often have company — up here near the clouds even my miserable hut appears like a mansion to someone seeking shelter. Who would enter my low door to squat on an earthen floor and partake of my wretched food if I lived in a village?"

"You are wise, grandfather," I agreed and smiled, "but have you no son who would give you a home?"

The old man shook his head and again bared his teeth in a grin. I noticed that two of the upper teeth were long like a dog's.

"Sons marry and have families of their own, and when the old ones are asleep the young ones begrudge them the corner they take up."

"You have not much use for your fellow men," Yoshitoki laughed. "Not all children wish their parents in their graves."

"No, those who have lost them when young," the old man shot a quick glance at the two of us, "can afford to proclaim that they love them. You!" He pointed a crooked finger at me. "You cannot remember yours, and you," he moved his finger to point it at Yoshitoki, "lost your father first and your mother not long ago."

"How did you know that?" I gasped, for it was true, Yoshitoki's mother had died that winter.

The old man did not answer but instead asked us if we wished to eat. Suddenly he became as businesslike as an innkeeper, even telling us the number of coppers our meal would cost; we did not bargain but agreed to his terms, which were not unreasonable. Putting more charcoal on the grate and fanning it until he got a clear flame, he began to cook. I glanced at Yoshitoki and he winked at me. I wondered if the old man were a demon, not a human being at all. Both bandits and demons in one day! I smiled to myself and stretched my legs. I was getting sleepy and, reluctantly, I felt my eyes closing and my head falling forward.

I must have slept for the better part of an hour, for when I woke up the food was ready. The old man handed me a black lacquerware bowl containing rice mixed with mushrooms and mountain herbs. As I ate I watched our host; beyond a shadow of doubt he was dirty and his fingernails were long and repellent to look at, but his eyes were alive and clever, and I felt that we were in no danger from him. I told him about the two monks we had met and warned him against them, should they visit him. The old man laughed disdainfully; obviously he felt no fear, but then to live here all alone in the mountain pass showed that he was no coward.

"Since you knew, grandfather, that my parents were dead, can you tell the future too?" asked Yoshitoki. When the old man did not reply immediately he added, "When will Lord Takeda rule Japan?"

"Never!" the hermit snapped. "He will die undefeated but he will never rule Japan!" The old man handed us each a bowl of miso soup; it was hot and warmed my inside. A wind had sprung up and the flimsy walls of the hut could not keep out the cold night air.

"It will be Lord Oda Nobunaga who will win," I said, not to the old man but to Yoshitoki.

"He, too, will fall." The old man bared his teeth. "The butterfly in spring does not know it will die in autumn; intoxicated by its own beauty it flutters from flower to flower, thinking that its life will last forever."

"How do you know all this?" I asked. I did not doubt his words, I merely sought an explanation. "Where can one read what is to come — in the stars?"

"In men's hearts their future is written," the old man replied.

"And what is written in mine?" Yoshitoki asked, staring stubbornly at our host.

"Who knows?" The old man looked away, refusing to meet my friend's gaze.

"You do, I think, but that does not matter." Yoshitoki nodded in my direction. "My friend here, will he, too, die young? Or will he live to dandle a grandson on his knees?"

"He will live to be old." The hermit looked sourly at me for a moment as if he regretted this fact, and then added maliciously, "But he will leave no-one to carry on his name."

"Will I become a samurai?" I asked, holding my breath as I waited for his answer.

"Oh, you will wear the two swords, both of you, as your fathers did, but it will do you as little good as it did them." The old man rose and went to the door to look out. "Soon winter will be here, snow will cover the mountains, and then the footprints of man will be rare."

"What is the weather like?" Yoshitoki had risen and was peering out behind the old man's back. "I think it will be pleasant," he said, answering his own question.

"As soon as it is light enough to travel, let us start," I suggested, for I was still a little afraid that the two bandits might catch up with us and I felt far from certain that we would be lucky in encountering them a second time.

"If you want to sleep, I shall waken you when the first light covers the peaks." The old man indicated the floor as our bed. When we lay down he brought out some old straw raincoats that we could use as covers.

It seemed to me that I had just fallen asleep when the old man woke us. He offered me a cup of soup and a rice-ball, which I ate greedily. The light outside was still gray but the mountaintops had a golden shine that promised well for the day. We paid the old man and he carefully put away the coins. When we mounted our horses he held the stirrup for Yoshitoki and bowed deeply as we left. I looked back as we rode away. The old hermit was returning to his hut and I noticed he walked so bent over that it was almost as if he were walking on all fours.

We reached Kofuchu the next day and delivered our message. We stayed in my old room in Lord Akiyama's mansion for two nights, and then started out on the return journey to Iida Castle. By an unspoken agreement we planned to enter the pass on the summit this time in the middle of the day. Neither of us had any wish to spend another night with the old man in his lonely hut. When we reached the summit we dismounted and tied our horses, feeling that we had at least to pay the old man a visit. To our surprise, the hut seemed more of a ruin that it had on the night we had stayed there. The door that I had seen the old man open and close was now gone, and so was the hermit himself. The place looked as if it had not been inhabited for a long time. The little grate that had held the charcoal fire was still there, but it lay on its side. I found one of the cups in which we had been served tea, chipped but still unbroken; I held it carefully in my hand and decided to keep it.

"He has left," Yoshitoki said without conviction in his voice. "No," I replied, "he was never here."

Yoshitoki nodded and sniffed the air. "Can you smell it? A fox or a wolf has been here."

"A vixen can turn herself into a woman," I exclaimed, "but not into an old man!"

"He was a demon." Yoshitoki's voice shook.

"Or a badger," I suggested, remembering the old man's teeth and his long clawlike fingernails.

"Badger, fox, or demon — but not human." Yoshitoki grinned. "We will have something to tell when we are back in Iida Castle!"

We stopped at the first house we came to and inquired about the old man who lived in the pass. We were told, as we had expected, that an old man had lived there once, but that he had died long ago. His grave, they told us, was at the back of the hut beside a large boulder.

We looked at each other and smiled, for it is not granted everyone to be able to say that they have been fed and have slept in the house of a ghost.

{12}

A Name, A Name!

On the last day of the year Lord Akiyama returned and the castle was again filled with life. But not all returned. I gave no thought to the missing ones, but envied the heroes who could brag of their experiences on the battlefield. There was much talk of when and how Lord Takeda Shingen would lead his armies toward Kyoto in order to make himself master of Japan.

Once when we had been listening to some samurai discussing this, Yoshitoki said, "They are like ravens waiting for corpses to feed on."

"Why do you say that?" I asked, surprised at the bitterness of his voice.

"They would like to see Japan ruled from Kofuchu because they come from Kai themselves. They have no thought for anything other than power and gold. They are greedy like ravens, and if Lord Takeda wins they will treat Japan like those birds do the corpses on a battlefield."

I nodded sagely but could not help protesting that I would not mind becoming the ruler of even the smallest of villages myself.

"You would like a name other than Taro?" he asked smilingly.

"Have you ever heard of a samurai named Taro?" I

countered, for it was very true that I wanted another name.

"Lord Takeda's name as a child was Taro, I have been told," Yoshitoki said.

"I did not know that." I was a little surprised that Lord Akiyama should have given me Lord Shingen's childhood name. The news pleased me, because I was always looking for omens of good fortune.

"Do you think I could beg Lord Akiyama for another name?" I asked, mentioning that he had once said that he would soon have to give me another.

"I would not push my luck too far." Yoshitoki shook his head. "To gain the attention of the great you must handle them like fishes that you want to catch. It takes even more patience to land a lord like Akiyama Nobutomo than an ayu."

I could not help laughing at his comparison, although I did not doubt its appropriateness. Oh, I thought to myself, I shall be ever so patient, but I shan't miss my chance when it comes. Too much patience can also lose you your fish.

That chance did not come for a long time, and I remained Taro when others my age, and even younger, had begun to be considered men and were given names appropriate to their ranks and stations. The following summer Lord Akiyama raised an army again and was away for a good part of the year. I was left behind, and this time Yoshitoki was among the gaily bannered squadron of cavalry, riding a little black mare that had been a favorite of us both. I waved to him but kept a stern expression on my face so that no-one should guess that I was near to tears. The night after the army had left, I decided that, should the same happen the following year, I would commit hara-kiri as the only honorable way out of my disgrace. It was easy for me to come to this decision when its accomplishment was a whole year away. I felt as brave as if I had indeed done it already, and before I fell asleep that night I imagined to myself the sorrow that Lord Akiyama would feel when he was informed of my sad and desperate act.

As soon as Lord Akiyama returned I would ask him for a name, but I would have to choose the right moment. It would not do to trouble him; that might make him angry. No, the time to ask would be when I had been sent for by him for some reason or another and could judge him to be in good enough humor not to mind. I spent all that summer rephrasing my request over and over again. Sometimes my demand seemed so reasonable that I did not doubt my eventual success, for had not Lord Akiyama already said that it was time he gave me a new name? But then black clouds would enter the blue sky, and in my imagination Lord Akiyama would not only refuse me a name but would punish me for my impudence by sending me back to the stables. I longed for Yoshitoki's return; I needed his advice and his friendship, for although the others were not unfriendly to me I felt isolated among them because of my accursed child's name. Taro, oh, how I hated the sound of that name and how desperately I wanted another!

When the army finally returned, I rushed to Yoshitoki, and, not even giving him the slightest chance to tell of his adventures, I blurted out my problem. Though he had taken off his armor and helmet he was still wearing his swords. He glanced down at one of them, then at me, and drawing it out so that I could catch a glimpse of its glittering blade, he said half sorrowfully, "It has killed several men. There are times now when I wish myself back to before I became Yoshitoki, when I was only a boy!"

I did not have any sympathy for what he had said. Scarcely understanding, I replied "You cannot become a boy again once you are a man."

Yoshitoki took off his swords; he had two, like a real samurai, though the second was very short and more like a dagger.

"You are right, it cannot be done. Only in dreams can you return to what you once were." He smiled bitterly and continued, "And though you can return you are like a ghost, powerless, unable to change what has happened. You can only experience once more what you would often prefer to forget."

"You are a samurai now," I said bitterly, "and I am nameless, for Taro is like a grain of rice — there are so many of them that they cannot be counted."

"Once Lord Akiyama spoke to me. It was after the battle. . . . He asked about you." Yoshitoki paused and smiled teasingly.

"What did he say?" I demanded. "Please tell me!"

"He asked what I thought of you," Yoshitoki said and grinned. "I told him and that is all."

"But he remembered me!" I said eagerly and then repeated, "He remembered me!"

"You didn't ask me what I replied!" Yoshitoki put his arm on my shoulder and we both laughed.

When I finally got a new name, it came about in the most natural manner. I was called to Lord Akiyama's chamber and, as usual, I entered and knelt just inside the room, awaiting my master's order.

"What was your father's name, Taro?" Lord Akiyama asked.

"I cannot remember, my lord," I whispered, and then taking courage I added, "But his family name was Murakami."

"Murakami." Lord Akiyama tasted the word and then repeated it. "Murakami . . . that will do . . . Murakami Harutomo . . ." Lord Akiyama smiled. "Will that satisfy you?" he asked.

I bowed while silently repeating the name, Harutomo. . . . The name was constructed from the place-name Haruchika, which Lord Akiyama ruled and which sometimes served him as a nickname among the other lords, and his own name Nobutomo. By giving me a name so closely related to his own, he had shown that I stood high in his favor.

"You do not answer. Is the name not to your liking?" Lord Akiyama knew perfectly well that my silence was one of respect and that I had not dared utter a word.

"It is a good name, a very fine name," I muttered and then bowing to the floor, I said, "And I thank you for it — it is a precious gift. But will it please Lord Takeda that I should be called Murakami?"

"He has long forgotten that name," Lord Akiyama laughed. "Do you not think that the future ruler of Japan, the Kai Shogun, has more important things on his mind than the name of a boy?"

"I did not want to offend," I whispered, realizing that I had indeed thought that Lord Takeda Shingen might remember my name.

"The center of each man's soul is the center of the world," Lord Akiyama said, laughing. "Even a beggar thinks that in his cupped hand he holds a universe." Lord Akiyama took a sword from behind him; its sheath was plain but it was no weapon to feel ashamed of. "It is customary to give a gift to someone when he is given a name. . . . Take this sword; it was won on the battlefield and belonged to a brave man."

I felt my face flush with pleasure as I knelt in front of my lord and received the sword. I held it in both my hands and then bowing I thanked my master, who dismissed me with a kindly nod and a wave of his hand.

"I am Murakami Harutomo!" I shouted as soon as I caught sight of Yoshitoki.

"A good name!" My friend grinned. "And before sunset there will be no-one in Iida Castle who will not have heard of it."

{13}

Rumors of War

*I*t is said that a loose tongue can outrun a horse. I do not know if this is true, but certain it is that what happened in Kofuchu was often known so swiftly in Iida Castle that one could hardly believe that a mountain range divided us from the town. In the house-laws of the Takeda family there are several warnings to the retainers not to gossip about the affairs of their lord. If Lord Shingen had made this the first, the last, and the only rule it would still have been disobeyed. There are few who do not like to gossip and fewer still who will not lend an ear.

That winter when I became Harutomo, the rumors flew so fast that after a while one ceased to listen to them. Their subject was always the same: Takeda Shingen's march to the capital. But the routes to Kyoto were many. Some said that we were to fight one final battle against Uesugi Kenshin and subdue the province north of us, in order not to be attacked from the rear. Other rumors had Lord Takeda planning an attack against two lords to the south. One thing all the rumors had in common was that they anticipated war, a final battle that would either make Lord Takeda Shingen ruler of Japan or mean the destruction of him and his family. If Kai were to be the new center of power in Japan, maybe even the seat from which the country would be ruled, then such glory awaited Kofuchu that even the thought of it could make any man move restlessly in his sleep.

Chief among the enemies of Lord Takeda was Oda Nobunaga. The two men shared the same ambition, to be ruler of Japan. Neither would acknowledge another as his equal, but Lord Oda had a cruel streak in his nature; he seemed to take pleasure in his own ferocity. Lord Takeda could be merciful, and an appeal to his clemency was not always in vain, but no-one need waste his breath in asking for Lord Oda Nobunaga's charity. Lord Takeda could be fierce and grim, but Lord Oda was merciless to his enemies.

The news that Lord Oda had attacked the temple of Heyeizan and destroyed the warrior monks there was taken as a declaration that he, too, was wiping out his enemies before he chose to make his final bid to subdue the country. The warrior monks and Lord Oda had long been enemies; now the great temple of Heyeizan lay in ashes and most of the monks and priests had been killed. It was said that the mountainside had resembled a slaughterhouse and that blood had run like rivers, a scene of such unbearable horror that those who had seen it would never forget.

"That will help us!" young Kenmotsu declared. "Now all the monks will know who their enemy is."

"But are you sure they will think us their friends?" Yoshitoki shook his head. "I cannot say I care much for those monks who seem to be more adept at swinging swords than reading sutras."

"The Ikko monks at Nagashima put Lord Oda to flight. They say that the monks beat his troops until they fled like curs that have felt the whip." Kenmotsu looked very wise and lowered his voice a little. "If I were our Lord Takeda, I would try to make them our allies."

"The Ikko sect have made our Lord Buddha into a foolish figure that no man who has ever had a thought in his mind could worship." Yoshitoki spoke with contempt. "Having found their own foolish road to salvation, they insist that we all have to stumble along their crooked path. Whether it is our Lord Takeda or our enemy Lord Oda who finally rules Japan, he will have to destroy the Ikko sect."

"Why are there so many sects? Why can they not all agree to the same thing?" I asked. When both Yoshitoki and Kenmotsu laughed, my face flushed as I protested, "But maybe there are many roads that lead to our Lord Buddha, and all may be equally good."

"No-one can own our Lord Buddha. That would be a foolish claim, but the roads that lead to him, the Way . . ." Yoshitoki laughed. "That is a different matter. They are all filled with toll-gates, like the roads of Japan, and the monks collect the fees."

"Zen is the only noble way." Kenmotsu's expression was serious and sober, indicating to us that this was a grave matter. "If I were ruler of Japan I would only allow two sects — Zen and the followers of Amida Buddha, the one for the samurai, the other for the rest."

"Then I am glad you are not Shogun." Yoshitoki shook his head. "I say let there be as many sects as people want.

If you must suppress a sect, let it be one that wishes to suppress others. As for myself, I think I will look for my own path."

"Why?" Kenmotsu looked at my friend in surprise. "Nearly all samurai practice Zen — it is the Way of Enlightenment."

"Possibly the light of Zen is so strong that it has blinded me to its virtue." Yoshitoki smiled.

"It is a very good discipline for the mind, as the martial arts are for the body." Kenmotsu looked very smug as he said this. "I do Zazen twice a week."

"I think it will do no-one any harm, though personally I find it more pleasant to think than to empty my mind of thought." Yoshitoki rose. We had been sitting on the castle wall looking at the town below us. "I shall not quarrel with another man's road to salvation if he will allow me to wander along mine. He may believe that all divine wisdom is found in the lotus sutra, or chant 'Namu Amida Butsu' like those of the Jodo sect for all I care."

Kenmotsu shrugged his shoulders as a sign that he gave Yoshitoki permission to believe in whatever he chose to, and walked away. When I was sure that he was out of earshot I turned to my friend and said, "All the same, it is very difficult to empty your mind of all thoughts. I have tried to do Zazen and couldn't."

"Possibly some people find it easier than others to empty their minds of thought," Yoshitoki suggested drily. "If all the high-ranking samurai of the Takeda army should decide to embrace the Pure Land sect, Kenmotsu would join and find it vastly superior to Zen."

I nodded in agreement but said nothing, for I recalled only too well my reason for attending Zazen at En-ko temple.

The following summer, in the eighteenth year of my life, the order finally came from Kofuchu for Lord Akiyama to assemble his troops. The period of waiting, the period of rumor, was over. Everyone felt a great relief, as if they themselves rather than Lord Takeda had made the decision to go to war. There was much polishing and sharpening of swords and repairing of armor, but little talk, as if the awesomeness of the moment had lamed everyone's tongue. We messengers carried orders far and wide; no sooner had one of us returned before he was sent away again. No magic word exists that can raise an army overnight; much planning and thought is necessary and I was surprised to find that Lord Akiyama was concerned with every detail. The collection of rice and millet to feed his army preoccupied him especially, and he would inspect personally the grain brought from the storehouses of his vassals.

Somehow I knew that I should not be left behind this time when the army left, but I was far from certain what part in the campaign would be mine. I had a sword but neither helmet nor armor. I wanted to be among the samurai who rode next to my Lord Akiyama, but, without equipment that would not shame both my master and me, that would not be possible.

{14}

"Master of Rice"

Lord Akiyama had gathered together more than two thousand warriors, and now his army awaited only the order from Kofuchu, from Lord Takeda Shingen. Iida Castle was so filled with people that at night you could hardly make your way through the rooms and corridors for sleeping samurai. It was late one evening that I was told to report to my master; I hastened to obey, for I expected to learn what my duties would be once the army had been ordered to move.

As soon as I entered the room I suspected what was about to happen, for seated next to Lord Akiyama was an elderly samurai named Wada Kansuke. He was the commander of the Konidatai, the baggage train, the horde of luckless peasants who guided the packhorses laden with rice, millet, and spare weapons and who carried heavy loads, like patient beasts of burden themselves. A week earlier I had served as his messenger when stores of rice and grain had been assembled. Wada Kansuke had a reputation for being a hard master and difficult to please, but I had not found him particularly so, and we had worked well together — a fact that now, as I knelt in front of my lord and bowed my head in submission, I feared had sealed my fate.

"For every samurai in helmet and armor, there must

be another man more humbly dressed. He leads a horse instead of riding it; both he and the beast carry burdens; he is as necessary as the proud warrior, though he probably does not know it." Lord Akiyama paused and looked at me searchingly. I met his gaze though I found his words far from pleasing. "You are to be the aide to this officer. There is none in the whole army I trust more than him. Obey him as you would . . ." For a moment Lord Akiyama's gaze fell on the old samurai seated beside him and I, too, looked at him. The skin of his face resembled leather that had been creased and worn, his eyes were mere slits. I had been told that his body was covered with scars, each marking some heroic deed. "Obey him as you would a father." A tiny, barely perceptible smile played on Lord Akiyama's face as he spoke the last word.

"It could have been worse." Yoshitoki laughed as I told him of my new position. "You could have been put in charge of the Shinshu and made to dig with a shovel." Yoshitoki was referring to the engineering troops who were used in building camps and when a castle was besieged.

"Why won't he let me fight?" I asked truculently.

"Possibly because he wishes that pretty head of yours to stay on your neck." Yoshitoki grinned. Although not dressed in armor he carried his helmet with him. "I would be pleased if someone in this world cared if I kept mine!"

"I do," I said, and meant it.

"Thank you." Yoshitoki smiled, but suddenly his expression grew serious. "You know, you will be a man of some importance; few care to quarrel with someone who can untie the rice sacks. I will be one among thousands, whereas you . . ." Yoshitoki paused and then held out his helmet to me. "Take this and I will trade with you!"

I laughed, for I knew it was impossible. "Do you think they will let me have a horse?" I asked naively.

"You won't be asked to walk." Yoshitoki shook his head. "It is a position of great trust. There are more than a few coppers to be made if you should prove dishonest."

"How?" I asked incredulously, for I had not thought of this.

"By selling our stores. There will be soldiers enough looking for rice, some because they are hungry, others because they are thirsty and want it for brewing sake. The latter will pay more than the former."

"Kansuke is honest, I am sure of that." I wrinkled my brow while I contemplated if I was.

"And that is why he is in charge of the baggage train. You will find enough brave men among our troops, but honest ones . . ." Yoshitoki laughed.

"I will try to be honest," I declared to my friend's amusement. "But I wish I weren't so poor," I added and laughed myself.

"That is true. Poverty is not the best condition for ensuring honesty. But if I were you, I would be careful to accept no gifts from anyone."

"Not even from Lord Akiyama?" I asked.

"Oh, from him it is safe enough, and should Takeda Shingen himself give you something, you may accept that as well." Yoshitoki put his hand on my shoulder.

"In all seriousness Harutomo, don't accept anything from anyone else."

I nodded. I was pleased by the seriousness of my friend's voice. I was no longer a boy, I was Murakami Harutomo, aide to the officer in charge of the baggage train of Lord Akiyama's army.

"Any news from Kofuchu yet?" Yoshitoki looked around him despairingly. The town of Iida was overflowing with soldiers. "If we do not get orders to move soon, we will have trouble breaking out among some of the troops. There was a fight last night between some archers and a group of foot soldiers. What it was about I don't know, but I suspect it was caused by boredom."

"Some high-ranking lord came last night. The sheath of his sword was inlaid with gold." I hesitated to say more. "His horse was panting and wet with sweat; he had come from Kofuchu." At that moment we were jostled by a couple of samurai who gave us a look of disdain as they passed.

"Fools," I muttered under my breath. "They think themselves better than an officer of the baggage train!" I still could not help but feel degraded by my new post, however important it might be.

"Has no-one offered to buy rice from you yet?" Yoshitoki asked in an effort to improve my humor.

"This morning someone did." I burst out laughing as I recalled the incident. "He was a foot soldier. Every time he saw me he bowed so low that I was afraid he might fall on his face. He didn't speak to me. He just bowed again and again as if his backbone were made of hinges. When I finally asked him what he wanted, he fell on his knees and touched the ground with his forehead before he spoke. 'Master of Rice' he called me and held out a handful of coins, begging me to sell him a measure of rice."

"What did you do, O Master of Rice?" Yoshitoki bowed, imitating the soldier.

"I told him to get out of my sight before I had him dragged in front of Lord Akiyama and that frightened him. He left walking backward, making small bows as he went. I had a hard time not to burst out laughing. Still, you know we have had to set guards around our depots, and even so a few rations of rice have been stolen."

"In some ways it will be easier once we are on our way. Most of the troops will be too tired to think of much else than sleep. Now they have nothing to do and they are bored; there is rivalry between some and bad blood between others. I hope your great lord with his gold laced sword brought news that we are to leave."

"He did! Tomorrow after sunrise." I lowered my voice to a whisper so that no-one else could hear me. "We have been ordered to issue each man three days' supply of rice and millet — that's how I know."

"But that is the usual ration, is it not? That does not mean we are leaving," Yoshitoki argued.

"We were told to give it out at sunrise, as the army would be leaving shortly after. We are to have everything packed and the horses laden before the hour of the dragon has passed."

"We shall be heading south toward Toutomi and Mikawa." Yoshitoki looked very wise and serious. "In Hamamatsu Castle in Mikawa rules Tokugawa Ieyasu — he is Oda Nobunaga's friend and ally. Lord Tokugawa is an able man, I have been told. After we have defeated him we shall turn towards Mino and fight Lord Oda himself, and when we have beaten him we shall enter Kyoto and Takeda Shingen will be ruler of Japan — the new Kai Shogun."

I shook my head. "We are not going south. Lord Akiyama's troops are heading towards Mino. We are to fight the Oda army and prevent Lord Oda from coming to the aid of Lord Tokugawa." I smiled, feeling very superior as I told my friend this.

"O Master of More Than Rice, how do you know all this?" Yoshitoki looked at me in surprise.

"Last night my captain, Wada Kansuke, had drunk a few cups of sake and he told me."

"Did he also tell you whether we would win or lose?" Yoshitoki grinned. "Though usually when people have drunk sake they are sure of victory!"

"Oh, we shall win!" I replied, for I felt sure at that moment that we would. "Having split them up like that, we shall certainly defeat them."

"And who are 'we'?" Yoshitoki laughed sarcastically. "Takeda Shingen may win. His army is great and powerful and he is an able general, but whether we shall win . . . that is a matter of which I am not so sure."

"What do you mean?" I asked, bewildered.

"In all great victories some soldiers of the victorious

army are also slain. . . . The corpses on the battlefield do not all belong to one side."

"Yes," I mumbled in agreement, although still not understanding what my friend meant.

"Those soldiers belonging to the victorious side whose blood has oozed into the ground and whose hearts have ceased beating, have they partaken in the triumph as well as those who are unscarred and busy draining cups of sake to each other's glorious deeds? I rather think they belong instead to the defeated. So let us not speak about 'we,' about you and me."

"You mean that those who are killed all belong to the defeated, regardless of which side they were on?" I asked. I had never thought of it like that. "Then each man is like an army by himself!" I exclaimed.

Yoshitoki nodded. "But even if we survive — you and I — and we enter Kyoto with our victorious general, all is not over. Then comes another fight, different from the one on the battlefield, not as dangerous but not as clean either. The sharing out of honors and prizes, the spoils of war, that is another battle for which even greater skill may be necessary." Yoshitoki grinned. "No, I shan't predict our fortunes before they are fulfilled. Many a victorious warrior has ended his day with a beggar's bowl in his hand."

Just at that moment someone called my name. It was my captain, Wada Kansuke. I smiled a little forlornly, for Yoshitoki's words had contained truths that I did not want to hear.

{15}

The Thief

"Keep your men together at all times. Don't let them mix with the warriors. There are some samurai who are not above offering bribes to get rice which they have no right to. Our men might try to barter it too for sake at some village. If you find any of the Konidatai drunk, tell me." Wada Kansuke narrowed his eyes to the point where you could hardly make out if he had any. "And if you catch any of our men selling the rice . . . kill them!" The old samurai snapped out the last two words in such haste that they became one.

"Yes," I agreed, even as I wondered if I could kill a defenseless man, regardless of his crime. The men who guided the horses carried heavy burdens themselves; I had found them a pitiable lot. They were so poor that I was sure that there had not been many days in their lives when they had gone to bed with a well-filled stomach. It was now the tenth month of the year and the night air could be bitterly cold, yet few of them had more than hempen rags to cover themselves with. Could one really blame such wretched creatures for being tempted to sell a few grains of the rice that they were burdened with?

It was as if Kansuke had guessed my thoughts, for he

suddenly added, "It is better to kill one man than to have to end the lives of ten. Once someone has sold rice and has gone unpunished, others will be quick to do the same; soon there will be little rice left. Then you will have to answer to Lord Akiyama. What will you say, what excuse will you give?"

"I shall do my best," I said, not answering his question.

"Best!" Wada Kansuke sneered. "Best may not be good enough! Without the rice these miserable worms are carrying there could be no army, remember that! I chose you because I thought you honest, but I am afraid you may have too tender a heart. A man's life is but the evening breeze that rises at sunset and makes the bamboo sway — it is nothing at all."

I bowed my head to show that I agreed, and suddenly the old samurai smiled and put his hand on my shoulder. "Keep your eyes open," he whispered. Then opening his eyes as wide as he could, he gave me an affectionate push in the direction of where the men were unloading the horses for the night.

Four days after we had left Iida Castle, the tenderness of my heart was tried. Certain men had been chosen as subleaders; Kansuke had made all the decisions save one, a young man named Denji, to whom I had given the post. He had been suitably grateful, a little too much so for my taste; when we camped at night he would run at my heels like a puppy seeking a master. I had also noticed that he took a little too great a delight in ordering others about. I was sorry that I had chosen him but reluctant to admit, even to myself, that I might have made a mistake. One evening after we had unloaded the horses and set up guards around the supplies, an elderly man among the Konidatai asked permission to speak with me. As I sensed that what he had to say might not be meant for ears other than mine, I indicated to him to follow me to a place where we would not be overheard.

"Master." The old man kneeled and bowed his head in shame as he said, "Some of my rice has been stolen."

"When?" I asked. For some reason I did not for a moment think that the man could be lying and merely trying to cover up the fact that he had sold it himself.

"I am not certain. Someone cut a hole in one of the bags my horse is carrying. The hole has been repaired, clumsily, but still I might not have noticed."

"How much was taken?" I asked.

"Not so much, a man's ration for maybe a week. But I thought it best to tell you."

"It was probably done at night," I mused, speaking to myself rather than to the man kneeling in front of me.

"I will keep watch tonight," he volunteered. "The thief may come back for more."

"If you could hide among the rice bales, that would be best," I suggested. "I shall keep watch myself." With a nod I indicated to the old peasant that he could leave; he rose and bowed twice before returning to the others. I glanced around me to discover if anyone had seen us, for if the thief had been listening we would be wasting a night's sleep by keeping watch. I saw no-one near me. As I returned Denji came rushing up to me, all but wagging the tail that nature had denied him. I was just about to inform him of the theft when something within me made me hesitate, and instead I told him to come along while I inspected the horses. Some of the beasts were already badly winded from carrying the heavy loads, and others were nearly lame. I ordered their loads to be changed, shifting some from carrying grain to toting arrows, spearheads, and straw horseshoes. It amused me that often the carrier who led the horse would be as pleased as though it were his own load that I had lightened.

In a few days the moon would be full; majestically it hung like a paper lantern in the sky. I had seated myself under a tree, not so near the bales of rice that it would be obvious that I was watching them, yet not so far away that I could not see them clearly. The old samurai's order to kill any thief apprehended was not forgotten, and I was ready to draw my sword as I sat waiting. The guards that we had posted would probably be asleep before long — you could not expect them to keep awake after a long day's march carrying heavy burdens. Several times I found myself dozing, my head falling forward on my chest. It was well into the hour of the tiger, so late that the moon had set, before anything happened. I must have fallen asleep again for I was awakened by a sharp cry and I jumped up, drawing my sword. Somebody was fighting among the rice bales, but as I came up the struggle ceased. The old peasant whose rice had been stolen had captured the thief and was holding him down by sitting across his chest. The captured robber, who had ceased fighting, was lying on his back staring up at me with frightened eyes. It was Denji.

At first I was so surprised that I could not speak; then anger possessed me, for I felt doubly betrayed. Somehow his slavish subservience now became an insult I could not bear, for it had hidden a scoundrel's heart. Grabbing a rope from a nearby packsaddle, I indicated to his captor to get up and leave Denji to me. Then, raising the rope, I brought it down as hard as I could. Again and again I swung the rope down on the cringing body of the thief, who moaned but did not scream in pain. At last I stopped, out of breath; Denji did not move, but lay still, looking up at me. I threw the rope back across the saddle I had taken it from.

"Make sure he carries a double burden of rice tomorrow." I turned to the older man who had caught Denji. "Let him carry your burden and someone else's as well. Should he stumble, use your whip on him as you would on a horse." Those we had chosen as subleaders led horses but carried no burdens themselves; by my order I indicated that I had chosen him to replace Denji.

"What is your name?" I asked.

"Yoichi," he said and smiled, revealing a toothless mouth.

"You did well. I am afraid I nearly fell asleep myself," I said, stretching the truth a little, and smiled. Then I walked away, trying not to notice the people who had gathered to watch the punishment.

"If you had killed him, you wouldn't be out of breath now," a voice near me said teasingly.

I turned. Wada Kansuke had watched it all. "Ah, but he was lying so near the rice that the blood would have spoiled it," I replied, realizing that at no point had I meant to kill Denji. The thought made me feel lighthearted.

"That would have been bad. It was very thoughtful of you, and, besides, a beating is more healthy both for the one who is receiving it and for the one giving it than is the stroke of the sword." The old samurai smiled. "Giving him a double burden to carry tomorrow was a very good idea. The beating and the double load will humiliate him and keep others from attempting to imitate his crime. I think it was wiser than to have used the sword. Your heart may not be of stone, but neither is it as soft as a woman's." With these words my commander left. I could hear him chuckling to himself in the darkness.

The night was growing pale; only the strongest of the stars were still visible in the sky, and soon we would have to start loading the horses again. On the mountainside the dying fires of the soldiers gleamed like the eyes of dragons. I could hear shouts of command; the army was leaving. I returned to my tree and was sitting watching the landscape slowly awakening to another day. A poem came to me, and for a moment I forgot all about Denji and what had happened.

Gentle is the night.
The morning light
Is too sharp for sight.
Batlike, I shall hide,
Waiting for the moon to rise.

The poem pleased me, although I was not sure if I understood it. I wished I had paper and brush and ink. A few days later I still recalled it and wrote it down.

{16}

The Ronin Bandit

"From now on don't drink from a well, only from rivers or streams. They will poison their wells." Wada Kansuke was speaking to a group of men of the Konidatai. "And don't lag behind. A straggler carrying rice is a temptation to bandits, and you may pay for your laziness with a slit throat."

We were now inside Mino, a territory ruled by Oda Nobunaga. So far the advance troops had had only a few skirmishes, and no serious battle had taken place. The baggage train was now guarded by a group of mounted soldiers; unluckily for me my friend Yoshitoki was not among them. We moved very slowly now and I thought it hardly necessary to warn anyone against becoming a straggler. When I expressed this view to Kansuke he grinned.

"Oh, I know that. I only wanted to scare those who might think of deserting. You complain that your horse has gone lame and let it rest; when the Konidatai are out of sight, you make for the hills, horse, rice, and all. But the thought of bandits lurking there will detain the more faint-hearted."

"If I were Lord Oda, I would attack the Konidatai and not bother to engage the army. Once we have been destroyed, Lord Akiyama would have to return to Iida for more supplies," I declared.

"It is well then for us that Lord Oda has not included you in his counsel." The old samurai grinned. "If he could, I am sure he would like nothing better than to destroy the baggage train. But the mountains protect us; a horse needs a road or at least a path to follow, and there is none but the one we are on. Lord Akiyama has thought of it and has given us soldiers for protection."

"They are more in the way than anything else," I complained, for the road was narrow and the soldiers who were supposedly for our protection often hindered our progress by pushing our men arrogantly aside. "They should stay to the rear of us only."

"Harutomo, Lord Akiyama should make you his general." The old samurai shook his head in mock wonder and then agreed with me. "The man in charge of our escort is not a friend of mine. If I suggested something to him, he would be sure either not to do it, or to do its opposite. We have quarreled before."

"You should tell him to make sure that his soldiers ride back and forth among our men at the narrowest points of the road, and if our heavily laden horses will not jump up the mountain like goats at their command, they should use their whips on them. Perhaps then he will order his men not to do this. . . . One of our horses has broken its leg."

"I know. She was an old mare, not of much use. I will try and say something to their commanding officer. I will try to be humble," Wada Kansuke said and laughed, "that is, if you will try to be patient! Whatever you do, don't get into a fight with them; some of them are hot-headed and may draw their swords."

I nodded and smiled. The old samurai and I had become fast friends in those few days since we started out from Iida Castle. We found that we actually agreed about most things; often Kansuke would search me out to give an order, only to find that I had already carried it out myself. "The sword fits the hand," Kansuke would say on these occasions and laugh.

Kansuke ordered me to make my way to the rear and hurry any stragglers, for it was known that bandits lived in the mountains. On my way I was jostled several times by mounted soldiers; once I was stopped and questioned as if I were a bandit by a samurai not so very many years older than I. I answered all his questions politely, while I repeated under my breath, "The answers of a wise man can make a fool angry, but the questions of a fool should not be able to anger a wise man."

When I reached the last of my men I had expected to find a troop of soldiers guarding the rear, but, to my surprise, there were none. The path lay empty in the sunshine as if no army had ever passed along it. I asked one of the stragglers if there were more farther back. He claimed that he was the last, but I did not trust him because he had looked down at his feet instead of at my face as he answered. I asked him why he could not keep up with the others and he gave the usual excuses, which I cut short, bidding him catch up with the rest or I would report him to Wada Kansuke. This threat made him hurry, and I watched him until the path turned and his horse disappeared among a clump of trees. Suddenly all the sounds of man ceased and the valley grew silent. It was strange to be alone when only a little while before I had been fighting my way through a river of men and horses. I sat on my horse as still as a stone Buddha, listening to the shrill cry of a bird and the drone of the wind through the branches of the trees. How long I sat like that I do not know; it was the tinkling of a chain on the bridle as my horse shook his head that brought me back to my duties.

Recalling the doubt I had felt when the straggler had told me that he was the last, I decided to find out if it was true. I kicked my horse into a trot and rode back the way we had come. I recalled that there had been a small brook shaded by trees and flanked by banks of green grass, a place to tempt a weary man to desert. I decided to ride as far as the stream. At one point the valley grew very narrow just before widening out; here a great rock stood beside the path like a sentinel. As soon as I had passed it, I knew I should be able to see as far as the brook, so I let my horse walk as I came near the huge boulder.

Oh, the man had been lying! I could see a laden packhorse grazing contentedly beside the brook, but where was the peasant? I was just about to make my beast trot when I realized that there were not one but two horses grazing, and the second horse was saddled. Was it one of our men, a bandit, or a samurai belonging to Oda Nobunaga? Which of the three could its rider be? There was not much chance that the man belonged to us. I debated whether to ride back and ask for help from our escort, but recalling how roughly I had been treated by them, I decided not to do so and spurred my horse into a trot ahead. I was halfway there before I saw the other rider watching me as he stood ready to mount his horse. As I came near I reined in my horse and drew my sword. I had no helmet, but my opponent was wearing one, and armor as well.

It will be an unequal fight, I thought. Yet I was not afraid; I recall thinking of Kansuke's words: a man's life is but the evening breeze. It made me smile.

"I am a samurai who lives in these hills, nameless as my master is now. Go in peace and ask not that I should bloody my sword on one so young!" The stranger had reined in his horse. He sat erect in the saddle, the blade of his sword gleaming in the sunlight.

"I am but young, my arm has not yet the strength of a grown man, nor have I a warrior's skill with my sword. My name is Murakami Harutomo; I serve my Lord Akiyama Nobutomo. I have come for the horse that is grazing near the brook — it is carrying rice that belongs to my master," I answered.

"Your lord has much rice and I have little." The samurai grinned. He was a ronin, a masterless samurai, probably a bandit.

"What happened to the man who was leading the horse?" I asked, while I prepared myself to fight, planning which way to attack my opponent.

"He was a deserter. He tried to sell me his rice and

horse. I paid him a traitor's wages, and now he may be reborn as a cockroach."

"Nameless one, prepare to follow him!" I boasted and spurred my horse. The ronin sat still in his saddle waiting for my attack, expecting me to pass him on his right. As I came near, I reined in my horse so sharply that it rose on its hind legs in front of his mount. Just as I had expected, his horse tried to turn in fear of my prancing mount. As I leaned forward and loosened the reins, my mare gained the ground again with all four legs and I brought down my raised sword and cut one of the reins of my enemy's horse. Suddenly he found himself pulling sharply on the one rein that was still connected to the bridle, and his horse immediately obeyed, turning away from me. For a moment the ronin was defenseless, his back towards me; I swung my sword once more and cleaved his right shoulder. He was wearing armor, yet my blow was forceful enough to wound him deeply and a rose of blood discolored the sleeve of his jacket. I heard his sword drop from his hand and fall with a clatter on the gravel of the path.

If he had tried to flee I would not have pursued him, but he made no attempt to escape. A little way down the path the ronin managed to make his horse stand still and he dismounted with great difficulty. I must have cut a tendon, for his right arm hung useless.

"So, Harutomo, you can brag to your lord that you have won a fight against someone whose sword is not unknown in Kai."

"I do not brag," I answered as I dismounted. "May I help you bandage your wound?"

"No!" The samurai tried to look at his shoulder, from which the blood was flowing in a steady stream. "I am tired of this life. The road to the west is the only one that may lead to peace."

"The road to the west is the road of death. Your wound may still be healed," I replied.

"I should have died with my lord." The man shook his head as if he were recalling some folly committed long ago. "There is a time in each man's life when death is right."

"Who was your lord?" I asked.

"Who?" The samurai smiled. His face was pale and I realized that it was many summers since he was born. I thought he was never going to answer but finally he replied, "Lord Obu. . . . You have heard of him?"

I nodded; only now did I realize that the armor of the samurai was laced with the red threads of Lord Obu's soldiers.

"Some people called him the Wild Tiger of Kai," I said.

The old samurai smiled as I mentioned his master's nickname. Lord Obu had sided with Lord Shingen's son Yoshinobu and had been killed like a common criminal.

"I should have proven my loyalty to my master by killing myself. But somehow each time my hand grasped for the dagger to commit seppuku, I found some reason to defer it."

"Let me bind your wound. I am sure my Lord Akiyama will allow you to serve him," I suggested.

"I serve Lord Obu and no-one else." The faltering voice of the old samurai was suddenly steadfast. "Would you have me be Katsuyori's servant? Yoshinobu was noble, even related to the Heavenly Descended, but Katsuyori is only a kept woman's child." The last words were sneered rather than spoken.

"So, Hanagata Minbu, we meet once more."

I turned. Behind me, still seated on his horse, was Wada Kansuke, a smile on his face. Like a young man he jumped from the saddle and, throwing the reins over the beast's neck, he left it untethered.

"Kansuke! It will be the last time we meet — the pup here has bitten me so hard that now there is no returning. But I would like to talk to you and ask you a favor, for the friendship we once shared."

"Minbu, what help can I be? The first temple I come to I shall ask the priest to hold a service for you, I promise that." Kansuke held up his hand as if he were holding a twig of purification in it.

"Tell the puppy that he can return to the kennel. He has done well, and once I am dead you may take my head and give it to him — he can send it to my Lord Shingen for a reward. But please leave us alone." Hanagata Minbu smiled toward me, and I noticed that the wound on his shoulder had almost stopped bleeding.

"Take the horse over there." Kansuke gave a nod with his head in the direction of the grazing packhorse. "Ride back and I will meet you later."

I ran and grabbed the lead of the horse and then mounted my own. Ready to set off, I paused for a moment, wondering how to say good-bye to a man who has chosen death. Finally, I put my hands in the position of prayer and bowed my head; turning to Kansuke I said, "I do not want his head. He was no enemy of mine or of my lord."

The ronin grinned and bowed his head in return, although I could see from his grimace that it hurt him to do so.

"Lord Takeda Shingen would have prized it, and Katsuyori even more. They would have put it over the gate of Tsutsujigasaki Castle for all to see."

I kicked my horse and rode away, without looking back. I wondered if the old ronin were not disappointed that I had refused his head, if in some way he would have liked it to make that last journey to Takeda Shingen. Man's vanity transgresses death; I had noticed that although he lived all alone out in the mountains, he had managed to blacken his teeth like a high-born samurai.

{17}

I Gain a Helmet

"This helmet is yours." My captain handed me the helmet that had belonged to the old ronin. It was a good one; at the back it came down almost to the shoulders, protecting the neck. "He wanted you to have it; he thought he had known your father."

I looked down at the head-piece in my hand. I had no recollection of my father and now I had killed or at least caused the death of someone who had known him. "Did he know my father's name?" I asked, for I only knew our family name.

"I did not think of asking him." Kansuke laughed. He was holding the reins of the ronin's horse as well as his own. Tied to the saddle of the horse was a bundle soaked in blood.

"I told you I did not want his head!" I exclaimed and tried to look away, but my gaze returned to that blood-soaked kerchief and what was inside it.

"That decision was not for you to make." Suddenly Wada Kansuke's voice was stern. "I will have it shown to Lord Akiyama. Whether it is worth the trouble to send it to Tsutsujigasaki Castle or not is up to him. Certainly one owes it to him that Lord Shingen should know. Hanagata Minbu fought four times at Kawanakajima. He was a most brave samurai."

Now I understood. It was for the sake of the ronin's honor that his head was now to be sent to Lord Shingen.

"He would want it?" I asked.

"Want what?" Kansuke looked at me in astonishment.

"Want his head sent to Lord Takeda," I stammered.

"Lord Shingen will have it buried and will let the priest in the temple hold a service and read a sutra for his sake. Naturally, he would like that."

"But he was Lord Takeda's enemy. One of Lord Obu's men," I argued.

Wada Kansuke laughed good-naturedly at my ignorance before he spoke. "Lord Obu revolted against Lord Shingen. That was a crime for which he was punished, for to revolt against your lord is the most serious offense that exists. He was a traitor, but his men — the samurai like Minbu who served him — remained loyal to him. That loyalty Lord Takeda Shingen will honor."

"Then I must remain loyal to Lord Akiyama, regardless of what he does — even if he is disloyal to Lord Takeda?" I asked.

"Certainly!" There was no shade of doubt in Kansuke's reply. "Your lord is like your father, you must follow him wherever he leads, even into death, to the road to the west."

"Lord Obu's brother was the one who informed Lord Takeda about the revolt that was being plotted against him. Whom should he have been loyal to?" I demanded. "Should he not have sided with his brother?"

"Yamagata Masakage is a brave man; he is the vassal of Lord Takeda, not of his brother. You must follow the lord whose service you are in as if he were your father —I have already told you so. Lord Yamagata did right in informing on his brother." Wada Kansuke sighed and shook his head. "Today there is little of that kind of loyalty. Everyone who can wield a rusty old sword thinks himself a samurai, and a hundred-koku samurai believes he is a great lord who need obey no-one but himself," he added bitterly.

"I obey you, and Lord Akiyama too," I said more lightheartedly and put the helmet on my head.

"Aye, a one-koku samurai." Kansuke grinned and mounted his horse. "I shall tell Lord Akiyama that you killed one of the bravest men of Kai. It will please him." With these words the old samurai gave his horse a kick and trotted away.

"It is a fine helmet. I have never seen better." Yoshitoki held my helmet in his hand; he touched the five plates of the neck shield reverently. "These will serve you well —so many helmets do not protect the neck as they should."

I nodded. I had received many compliments since my encounter with the vassal of Lord Obu, to which I had replied that luck had served me more than skill.

"I am not afraid," I mumbled.

"I did not say or think so." Yoshitoki looked at me in surprise.

"I wasn't afraid, I mean. I rather enjoyed the moment before I attacked, even the thought that I might be killed excited me, I found." I looked at my friend questioningly.

He nodded and said, "I know — I have felt the same before a battle."

"But afterward . . ." I paused, not knowing how to phrase what I wanted to say. "When I was a stable-boy we sometimes used to fight with bamboo swords, and when an opponent had been declared 'dead,' I felt . . ."

"Victorious," Yoshitoki interrupted with a smile. "I know. That feeling of victory can escape you when you see the blood of defeat rushing from a wound."

I nodded. "When you take someone else's world away from him, you feel the loss so strongly. That surprised me; I had not expected it."

"You feel it because you still have your world, in which the sky is blue and the sun shines." Yoshitoki's features were grave.

"Besides, you don't hate the man. . . . You probably don't even know him." I wrinkled my brow as I recalled the arm hanging loose from the shoulder, dangling like a broken branch. "I think I even liked the old man."

"Yet I tell you, Harutomo, he would have killed you and wiped his sword and forgotten he had done so before it rested in its sheath. The first man killed is like the first woman slept with — unforgettable." Yoshitoki laughed as he said the last cynical words. I agreed, though I was hardly the one to know the truth of what he had said. I had killed a man, but as for loving a woman . . . I wondered if Yoshitoki had, but I did not dare ask him for fear he would laugh at me.

* * *

"So, I have been told that you have proven yourself in battle." Lord Akiyama was seated on his horse; out of vanity, I think, he always rode a stallion. This was a magnificent beast, black like the night, with eyes of fire. I bowed my head in agreement but said nothing; my lord was accompanied by several of his retainers, all men of great importance. I guessed that Lord Akiyama had spoken about me, for they all looked at me with interest.

"It was a pity that he died. I would not have minded counting him among my men."

"I only wounded him, sire. I wanted to bind his wound and told him that I was sure that it would please you if he would serve you. He died by his own hand, not mine," I added modestly.

"And what did he say to that suggestion? It did not please him?" Lord Akiyama's horse moved restlessly.

"My lord, he said it meant that he would have to serve Katsuyori." I lowered my voice to a whisper. "And that did not please him."

"Loyal to the ghost of Yoshinobu," Lord Akiyama sighed. "More foolish than wise, he was. But loyal to Obu and to Obu's folly. I will include news of his death when I next send a messenger to Lord Takeda. Neither shall I forget to tell him who caused it. . . . I shall have his head buried at Iida, and I will tell the priests in the temple to pray for him."

"Thank you, my lord." I stood with my head bowed, holding my newly won helmet in my hand. I was pleased that the old samurai's head would be buried properly and not sent to Lord Takeda.

"Where is Wada Kansuke?" Lord Akiyama looked around searchingly. My captain, who had been standing near one of the horsemen, took a step forward.

"I am here, my lord," he said. He, too, had uncovered his head and was holding his helmet in his hands.

"You knew Minbu well?" Lord Akiyama pulled a little too hard on the reins and his mount moved backward into another rider's beast.

"We were friends once. In one campaign we fought together and slept side by side."

"But then something happened? Did you become enemies?" Lord Akiyama had brought his stallion under control again.

"No, we did not become enemies; we were just not friends any longer." Wada Kansuke wrinkled his brow as if he were trying to recall exactly what had happened. "Maybe I felt instinctively what was about to happen, though I do not ever remember him talking about Yoshinobu, or giving a hint of the revolt."

"Tomorrow we shall be near Iwamura Castle. When night comes, I want many fires burning. Let them believe that we are more than we are. I want the Konidatai to act as if they were soldiers, too — when the horses are unloaded let some of them ride them. From a distance they will not be able to see which men are soldiers."

"I shall have them blow the conch trumpet too." Wada Kansuke grinned. The trumpets made out of great conch shells were used to convey messages of command to the soldiers. Lord Akiyama laughed, then spurred his restive horse and galloped away, followed by his retainers.

{18}

The Strategy of War

"Will it fool them?" I asked my captain. We had ordered the men of the Konidatai to form groups of three and light fires. Now the narrow valley and the hillside looked as if they were mirroring the star-filled sky.

Wada Kansuke shrugged his shoulders and looked toward Iwamura Castle on the peak of the mountain. "It is one of the best castles in Japan, with plenty of water and several walls of defense. One thing is in our favor, though; they are many, too many, within its walls."

"Too many?" I echoed. I could not understand how there could be too many soldiers.

"Lord Akiyama burned one of the villages we passed through, you remember." Kansuke smiled. He knew perfectly well that I had not forgotten — the sight of the burning houses had angered me.

"I remember . . . also the dead oxen and the old woman who sat crying by the embers of her home." I looked angrily at the old samurai. "Why was it done? There was no reason for it."

"We have only two thousand men. There may be as many in the castle; but even if there are only five hundred men who can wield a sword, it will not be easy for us to conquer it. That is why the villages were burned —

Lord Akiyama sent out troops to burn others that you did not see. He wanted not to kill but to frighten the peasants and to drive them from their homes."

"Why?" I still did not understand the reason.

"Like a herdsman who drives a flock of oxen, he wanted them all inside Iwamura Castle: women and children with hungry bellies, clamoring for food the moment they passed the castle gate. You see, up there, too, they have fires." Kansuke pointed toward the crest of the mountain where the red glow from the fires could be seen. "They have many guests but none that they want, for they are the type of visitor that brings only an appetite to the party." Wada Kansuke grinned.

"And that is why we burned the villages!" I exclaimed. I was pleased that there had at least been some reason why the homes of the poor peasants had been destroyed. The old woman whom I had seen weeping had been too old to flee.

"War is like a fire. It spreads and consumes all in its way." Kansuke coughed and spat on the ground.

"When does it stop?" I asked, wondering if I should go down to where the cavalry was camped and look for Yoshitoki.

"When — like a fire — it burns itself out." The old samurai picked up a piece of wood and threw it into the the blaze; it sent a shower of sparks into the sky. "I don't remember when there has not been a war somewhere. My father, like yours, died in the first battle against Uesugi Kenshin. . . . But I was not a child then as you were when your father was killed."

"When will this war burn itself out?" I stepped back a little. The flames were hot, and I was getting scorched.

"Soon, I should think." Kansuke pointed into the fire. "The hotter it gets and the higher the flames, the sooner it will become ashes. We live in a time that men will talk about when we are long since turned into Buddhas."

"I doubt if you and I will become Buddhas." I grinned. "I think it more plausible that we will be reborn as . . ." I could not think what we should be reborn as, so I paused.

"If it must be an animal, let it be a horse," Kansuke said drily.

"I will choose a fox." I laughed. "A horse might be a packhorse in the Konidatai."

"The fox is near to the gods — it can change itself into a human being." Kansuke shook his head and scrutinized me for a moment before saying, "You will make a tanuki, that's all."

"A badger who drinks sake and does nothing all day but make mischief," I said, and laughed. "I shan't mind that."

"Sometimes I think that if I live long enough I shan't die but turn into a stone jizo." The old samurai looked at me seriously and, in truth, his features did take on the immobility of one of those small, crudely made stone images. What did he believe in? I wondered to myself. He worshipped at any temple or shrine, or at least bowed in reverence as he passed its gate. He treated me not so much as a son, but as if I were his grandchild and he was allowed to indulge me. Someone had told him that

I had turned back to look for stragglers that day on the pass, and he had been frightened that some harm would come to me and had galloped to my aid. Wada Kansuke had two needs in his life: someone above him to serve and worship and someone else to care for and protect. I served the second need, and Lord Akiyama the first.

Later that night I searched for Yoshitoki. The cavalry was camped closer to the castle. They, too, had been ordered to build as many fires as possible. From the summit of the mountain the enemy must have thought that it was an army of at least ten thousand that had come to attack them. I did not find my friend but stumbled across Kenmotsu sitting with two other young samurai near a fire. I was not particularly pleased to see him, but I smiled and bowed as he mentioned the names of his friends. They had a gourd of sake that they were passing among themselves. They offered me some, and I took a sip of it. It was not good sake and, besides, sake tended to make my face imitate the color of the sun as it rises above the horizon in the morning, so I quickly handed the gourd on to the others. Kenmotsu joked about me, saying that I had rice enough in my charge to brew as much sake as there was water in Lake Suwa. I grinned, and to my surprise one of the young men took it seriously enough to offer to purchase rice from me. I turned his demand into a joke, as if I did not believe that he had asked me in all seriousness. When he persevered I suggested he should ask my captain, Wada Kansuke, though I said I knew what his answer would be.

"And what would it be?" the young warrior asked.

"He will sell the rice entrusted to him by his lord the day the rest of you will sell your swords." I had heard Kansuke give that answer to a samurai who had only hinted that he would like to buy more rice than his ration.

The young man laughed. Kansuke's words had pleased him, for he patted his sword as if it were alive and understood what had been said.

"A samurai's sword is never for sale," Kenmotsu said pompously, while with his stick he drew out from the fire a sweet potato he had been roasting.

"Never?" I asked, hiding a smile and wishing that Yoshitoki were here to make fun of him.

"If he sells his sword he is no longer a samurai. A samurai without his sword is nothing." Kenmotsu peeled his yam; it was so hot that he was burning his fingers. He had not even understood what was meant, and I shook my head in wonder.

"How much rice do we have — how much and for how long?" the third young man asked.

"More than they have up there." With a nod of my head I indicated whom I meant. "They are many, and more than half of them are women and children who can eat but cannot fight." I went on to explain the strategy of the burned houses. Although I was pleased to find ears so willing to listen to me, as I held forth I was disgusted with myself for doing so. I did not particularly like these young warriors, I felt no kinship with them, yet here I was, trying to impress them with my knowledge.

A young warrior had made fun of the old woman who had sat so grief-stricken by the ashes of her home; it had not been one of these three samurai, but suddenly I felt as angry as if it had been. I refused another drink of sake and made my way back towards the small hillock where the Konidatai had camped.

I climbed to the very top of the hillock. The moon had come up and I sat on a tree-stump and watched its flight through the night sky. When I had been a poor boy working in the stable, or before that in the cookhouse with Togan, I had had only one dream — to become a samurai. Now I was one, even a trusted one, for Yoshitoki had been right: as aide to Wada Kansuke I was respected beyond my age; even older samurai treated me courteously. Only a few of the young ones, or the poorest of the bushi, thought themselves above me. So, I said to myself, your dream has come true; the gods have heard you and have given you what you asked for. Yet you are not satisfied. Why is that? I smiled a little forlornly — it was strange to be sitting here in the night holding a conversation with myself. "Because I was poor once," I whispered. "Part of me still belongs in the cookhouse with Togan."

I recalled the archery contest held when Katsuyori had become head of the Suwa family. I had run out in my rags as if I belonged among the young masters, and an attendant had roughly pushed me back among the watching servants. I was more properly one of them then than I am now, I thought. I shall always be not one but two persons.

A cloud had obscured and passed the moon, which

again threw its pale light over the landscape. The moon and the stars are constant; it is within ourselves that change takes place, and that is why we admire that lantern in the sky at night. I tried to make a poem, imagining that someone like myself was also watching the moon from within the besieged castle. It did not altogether please me, but if I only included in this story those poems that I thought good, it would be as if I told only of the times when I acted bravely.

So still, the world barely breathes,
The moon has painted with silver
The castle on the mountaintop.
Who within it has the calmness of heart
To watch the star-filled night?

{19}

The Ninja

The siege of Iwamura Castle was in its second week. No attack had yet been made nor had any defender sallied forth. The ring around the fortress was now so solid that no-one could escape or break through with messages. We knew that the besieged had water enough; there were good wells inside the castle. It would not be from thirst but from hunger that the castle would fall.

Wada Kansuke and I were kept busy distributing rice and millet to the soldiers. They had been divided into three groups and each in turn was given a ration that was to last for three days. This meant that every morning, just after sunrise, we served out grain. The food was scanty enough, and the soldiers made raiding parties on neighboring farms and villages to augment it. Often some soldier would have his ration stolen by someone hungry enough to rob a friend; then he would come complaining of his hard luck to us. When I thought it real hardship, I would sometimes manage to give him a little, at the same time making him promise to keep it secret — I feared that once it became known that I could be cajoled into giving extra rations, the whole army would come begging.

This was not our only function; after all, the Konidatai carried more than provisions of food. A foot soldier who had been in many battles and had experienced many sieges was in charge of the grappling irons and saw to it that the ropes attached to them were securely tied. To be able to swing such an iron up across a wall took not only great strength but also skill, and not everyone could do it. Once the iron hook has caught, one has to be quick to climb up the rope, for the defenders try to cut the rope and send you sprawling down again. These grappling irons, ropes, and all extra weapons were in our charge. We had made a depot for all our stores but, unfortunately, the only houses nearby had been burned by troops too eager to show their valor. What worried Wada Kansuke more than anything else was the possibility of rain, and he had had some makeshift huts made to store the grain. They would not have kept out a downpour, but so far we had been lucky and had had no rain.

In a way, I had come to like being with the Konidatai rather than being an ordinary samurai. As Yoshitoki had said, I would merely have been one of many and, at that, one of the youngest, whom everyone surely would have felt he had a right to order about. I was growing up fast — each day taught me something new about men and how to handle them. Wada Kansuke was a good teacher; he was ever patient but, at the same time, immovable when he thought himself in the right. Many of the Konidatai thought him a hard master but, in truth, he often defended them against others. But he was a proud man and neither joked, nor even talked, to the luckless farmers who made up our men, except to give them orders. He was concerned about them in the same way that he was about the horses — without the beasts and men to carry the packs there could be no army, so it was important that both horses and men were in a condition to carry out their tasks. To Wada Kansuke, a samurai and a farmer were so different that he never for a moment would think of comparing them. He expected the peasant to work, to labor until he was exhausted, but he did not demand from him the loyalty he expected from his own kind. If a farmer in the Konidatai had found life too hard to bear, Kansuke would not have thought it strange should he have drowned himself or hanged himself from a tree. But if the luckless one should decide to end his life by imitating a samurai and committing seppuku according to the sacred rituals, Kansuke would have considered such an action an intolerable insult to his honor.

I did not see Yoshitoki often. When I was free it was mostly at night, and he would often have to stand watch somewhere. But one evening we managed to be together. Wada Kansuke, who liked his sake though he hardly ever showed that he had been drinking, had a large gourd filled with this life-giving water. I had boiled some rice so there were rice-balls to eat. We sat near the fire, for it was now the eleventh month and the nights in the mountains were cold. The sky was clear and the moon nearly full — it was a proper moon-viewing party. Flushed from the sake and more daring than I was usually, I declaimed the poem I had made a few nights before and, to my surprise, Kansuke complimented me on it. I had not known that he liked poetry. He quoted a poem about the moon; whether it was his own or not I am not sure. I suspected it had been composed by a woman, and after the old warrior recited it he grew silent, as if he were traveling back through his life to some memory from his past.

It was nearly the hour of the rat when a guest joined our little party. In the middle of the night most of those who were not on guard duty were asleep, and all the world was quiet. We did not notice the newcomer, so silently and stealthily did he creep into our circle. It was not until he spoke that we saw his black-clad figure.

"Kansuke, have you a little sake for a friend?" His voice was thin, and as he sat there by the fire he reminded me more than anything of a bat. Kansuke shook the gourd and handed it silently to the stranger. Our guest repeated his host's movement, shaking the gourd first as if to make sure that there was indeed sake in it. He took a long draught, after which he wiped his lips with his hand and returned the gourd to Kansuke.

"Where have you come from?" my captain asked. With a movement of his head the man clad in black indicated the mountain and the castle behind him.

He is a ninja, I thought as I scrutinized the man. He did not wear a sword but a short dagger in his sash and some other weapon that I could not recognize; it was difficult to see as he was wearing a black, or dark blue, hunting jacket that almost covered it.

"And what was it like?" I tried to guess from Kansuke's face how much or how little he liked the stranger. Some people disliked ninjas and did not consider them proper samurai. I rather suspected that this would be my captain's opinion. His face was turned toward the spy, but his countenance was as stony as when people asked for more rice than they were entitled to.

"Lord Toyama is dead!" The ninja held out his hand toward Kansuke, who silently passed the gourd back to him. This, indeed, was news; that the governor of Iwamura Castle was no more could not help but aid our cause. "He died one week before we came — a fever took him." Again the ninja drank; this time at a nod from Kansuke he handed the gourd to me. I took a sip; there was little left and I handed it to Yoshitoki. He held it in his hand as he looked spellbound at the ninja.

"I would not have dared," he told me later. "To fight openly — yes, but to creep in like a shadow in the night — no, I could not have done it."

"Who governs the castle now?" Kansuke held out his hand to Yoshitoki, who handed the gourd to him without drinking from it.

"Lady Toyama." The ninja grinned, and in the moonlight his teeth gleamed: they were not painted black. "Oh, there is some other captain in command, but he would not dare to issue an order without a nod from Lady Toyama first."

Kansuke frowned, and I could not help thinking to myself, He does not approve.

"Why is this woman so obeyed?" he asked.

"There runs the same blood in her as in Oda Nobunaga. Again the ninja grinned. "She is his aunt but, I think, a few years younger than her nephew." I held out a rice-ball to our guest; he took it and popped it into his mouth.

"Oda Nobunaga is a handsome man. What is she like?" Kansuke held out the gourd to the ninja. He took it, pausing for a moment while he swallowed the last of the rice and then emptied the gourd before he spoke.

"I did not see her, but all of that family are handsome. They told me she is very beautiful; some thirty-odd times she has seen the snow of Mount Fuji melting in the spring."

"How did you get into the castle?" Yoshitoki asked timidly, more awestruck than was usual for him.

"When the poor farmers rushed to the castle in order to escape from the murdering Kai samurai, there was an old man among them more wretched than the rest." The ninja made a sudden movement and turned toward Yoshitoki. Then his face changed; suddenly he became old and his eyes took on the vacant look of one who has outlived his reason. It lasted only the briefest of moments, then he laughed and slapped his thigh.

It is magic, I thought and wondered if he were indeed human — could he be a badger or a demon? I looked at my captain, but his face wore its usual stony expression. The ninja handed him the empty gourd, then he rose and bowed deeply. The old samurai acknowledged this by a mere inclination of his head. As the ninja was swallowed up by the night, Kansuke took the gourd and threw it behind him as if he would never use it again.

"Who was he?" Yoshitoki asked. "Where did he come from?"

"From Sagami, I think." Wada Kansuke stirred the fire. "I think he is called Ietsugu. I do not know his family name." The stick the old samurai was using to poke the fire had caught fire itself, and he held it up for a moment like a torch. "Who knows whether that is his name; it could also be something else. . . . A ninja does not need a name."

"Lord Takeda uses many ninjas — I have seen them in Kofuchu." Having guessed that Kansuke did not like the ninja, Yoshitoki was careful not to point out that Lord Akiyama also employed them.

"How can one trust a man who lives by treachery?" Wada Kansuke threw the smoldering stick into the fire. "They may be useful. Certainly, it is important news that Lord Toyama is dead," he admitted grudgingly.

"They are very brave." Yoshitoki stretched himself.

"Brave?" Kansuke nodded as if he were answering his own question. "Yes, they are brave, I suppose. But they are also born traitors. Every ninja has had many masters, they serve for . . ." Wada Kansuke spat out the last word — "gold!" Then he rose as if he no longer wanted to discuss the subject with us and lumbered off into the night like a tired old badger going home to his cave.

{20}

A Trap Is Laid

Lord Akiyama often came to take counsel with Wada Kansuke; there was no doubt that he thought highly of the old samurai. When he saw me he would always greet me in so friendly a manner that it contained the overtones of familiarity used by an older kinsman to a younger. This was not lost on the retainers who attended him, and they in turn acknowledged this by treating me, although I was so much younger, almost as an equal.

Early one morning he sent a messenger bidding my captain to come to him. He had made his headquarters in a hut that, though damaged by fire, had not been so destroyed that it could not give shelter. When Wada Kansuke returned even his stony face could not hide a smile.

"We shall be retreating," he declared. "The Konidatai will be moving out in the evening, together with most of the troops. Only a small force will be left to keep the siege."

"Why?" I gasped. "They are already starving. They had no food worth eating when we came, and now there are twice the number inside the castle."

"Lord Akiyama has ordered a general retreat. A few of the cavalry and bowmen will be left to guard the place."

"Is this an order from Lord Takeda?" I asked.

"No, it is Lord Akiyama's plan." Kansuke looked down at his hands and rubbed them together as if he were washing them.

"Whoever is left behind is sure to be attacked!" I exclaimed incredulously. "And if they are few they will be killed too!"

"We hope they will be attacked, but not killed." Wada Kansuke smiled.

"But if they are only a few mounted men and some bowmen, how will they withstand an attack?" I argued.

"By retreating and drawing the attackers with them until the whole of our forces can fall upon them."

"Oh, it is a trap!" I said, beginning to understand why the call for a retreat had not made him downhearted. "Then we are not really to retreat?"

"The Konidatai will retreat so far that they are out of sight. This will be done with much shouting and screaming of command. Then" — the old samurai allowed himself a grin — "we will see what happens."

"What if nothing happens? If they suspect our trap?" I asked.

"I think they will be only too eager. The rumble of their hungry stomachs will be so loud that it will drown any whispers that prudence may make." Kansuke looked up at the sky; there were a few clouds. Immediately I understood why: this meant loading the rice on the horses once more, and what if it should rain?

"I think you are right, they will probably attack. Especially if it is true that Lady Toyama rules the castle — women know little about military matters," I said smugly.

"That is the only thing that has me worried." The old samurai shook his head. "I hope some young captain is in charge who wishes to earn Oda Nobunaga's gratitude, because then we are sure of their falling into our trap."

"But not if Lady Toyama rules?" I asked in surprise.

"Even a great lord's wife will search for a needle lost among the mats on the floor. Women are never wasteful. We men often are, though sometimes we hide our wastefulness by calling it generosity. A woman thinks three times before she parts with anything, be it a needle or a body of troops." Wada Kansuke paused for a moment, then, with a shrug of his shoulders, he said, "But then, she is of the Oda family and they are a headstrong, self-willed lot who do not know patience. So she may attack us even though she is a woman."

By afternoon the horses were laden, and the hut in which we had stored the rice was empty. During the night a group of archers was to hide there. The idea of making our retreat during the day was partly to emphasize its suddenness, making it appear almost a flight. It would also give us time to hide as many of the troops as possible under cover of darkness. When the first section of the Konidatai was ready to leave, Lord Akiyama arrived accompanied by five high-ranking samurai. He was eager to inspect the hut to see how many men could be hidden there. As he was ready to leave, a thought suddenly struck him and he called back Wada Kansuke whom he had just dismissed.

"We must leave a small group of the Konidatai, just to make them think that there is still rice left in the hut. Take twenty of the youngest and give them each a short spear. Then tell each man to hide it in a place where he can find it quickly when the time comes."

"Who shall be left in charge of them?" Kansuke asked.

"You can make that choice." Lord Akiyama frowned, then as he saw me he called my name, "Harutomo!"

I ran to obey. Standing at his stirrup on the right side of his horse, I looked up at my master; his helmet and armor were as splendid as they should be. "Since you have taken to fighting and wish to be a soldier, I shall leave you in charge," he said. Turning to Kansuke he added, "Find twenty young men who do not have the hearts of rabbits but of men. Let them walk about freely as though they have business to attend to, entering the hut where the rice was stored every once in a while as if they have some duty to perform there. Let Harutomo be left in charge — it is about time he heard how an arrow sounds when it whistles through the air."

"We shall find twenty of the best — there are some who are as brave as bears. . . ." Wada Kansuke was standing beside me. "But would it not be best if I stayed here too?"

Lord Akiyama laughed as he looked at the old samurai. "You have survived so many battles, yet you thirst to try your luck once more?" Lord Akiyama shook his head in dismay. "I shall not let you, for, in truth, I need your head more than your arm, your wisdom more than your courage, though I do not doubt the latter. You will lead the retreat of the Konidatai and stay with them."

"As you say, my lord." Kansuke bowed his head, sorry that he could not stay yet proud of the words his master had spoken in the hearing of all men. We watched them ride away. The standard bearer who held Lord Akiyama's flag was mounted on a bay mare that the lord's stallion obviously had a liking for; this often caused difficulty.

"I am sorry he would not let me — I would have liked to stay with you." Kansuke frowned as he looked up at the castle. "If you are on horseback, always attack another rider from the left and slightly behind, then you are stronger and he weaker. If you are on foot, go for his beast and do not ever attack from the front or he will hack you down. His armor may protect him, but it also makes it difficult for him to turn in the saddle, so attack him from the rear and he will be at your mercy."

I nodded, signifying that I had understood and agreed, although I had scarcely been listening, so proud was I of my commission. The old samurai did not notice, but went on to give me more advice.

"Take a good short spear with you — it is the handiest weapon when fighting gets close, better than the sword. Cook yourself a helmetful of rice tonight. Eat some and make rice-balls of the rest for tomorrow, and make sure that the men do the same. Don't let them eat it all tonight or their bellies will be heavy in the morning."

Wada Kansuke stopped and looked around as if he had only just become aware that most of the Konidatai had already left and that it would be best to choose quickly those men who were to stay behind.

"Yoichi!" The old man looked up at me and smiled; he was crouching by the fire watching the rice he was cooking. "You did not mind staying?"

"No, master," he answered and his reply made me smile. We had only built two fires. The other, not far away, was bigger and around it sat the men whom Wada Kansuke had selected. Although I did not think that he would be much help if it came to fighting, I had asked Yoichi to stay. I looked toward the place where the men whom the "retreating" army had left behind were camped. They, too, had been sparing in building fires.

I wonder what they are thinking up in the castle, I thought. They will be holding a council of war tonight. Will someone say it is only a trick, that they are trying to fool us? And if someone does, will he be believed?

I glanced toward the cooking rice; it would soon be ready. I rose and walked into the darkness. In a little while the moon would rise beyond the mountains. Suddenly a voice barked at me, "What is the password?"

Swiftly I drew my dirk as I shouted back, "And who asks it?"

"Someone who has a right to!" the voice growled. Three figures emerged from the darkness, and I recognized Lord Akiyama as one of them.

"The boar's tusk," I said, for that was the password.

"Why would you not speak up when first challenged?" Lord Akiyama asked.

"I thought it could be a spy from the castle who wished to learn it, my lord," I answered as I put away my dirk.

"Very well." Lord Akiyama nodded to indicate his approval. "But stay with your men. I will not have everyone running around like fleas in a beggar's rags." With these words, my master stepped into the gloom of the night once more, and I hastily returned to my fire, wondering what the ninja had been doing in the company of Lord Akiyama, for it was he who had challenged me.

{21}

A Sortie of Death

Iwamura is a fortified mountain standing on a plain. It has two walls of defense. The first encircles the base of the mountain and, near its gate, Lord Akiyama had posted archers who could shoot their arrows at heads peeking above the castle walls. In the general retreat, these soldiers were withdrawn. By morning, all that was visible from the castle peak were my men near the rice store and twenty horsemen detailed to protect us. Farther away, to the right of us, was another small detachment of mounted samurai, archers, and foot soldiers carrying spears; to the left of us was a detachment no larger. There were in all less than two hundred men.

The plain of Iwamura has many small hillocks and patches of forest; behind these small hills and among the trees Lord Akiyama had hidden his army. The few houses left in the village of Iwamura had been burned during the night as a departing army might do. The Konidatai had truly "retreated" and were now encamped among the foothills of the mountain range that surrounds the plain. I thought the invitation to attack us a little too obvious and expressed my doubts that the besieged would be foolish enough to accept it to the young commander of the mounted soldiers.

"Ah, but you do not know how hungry they are!" he

exclaimed. "Not only for food, but to fight us as well. They are packed like silkworms and have no mulberry leaves to eat!" He laughed, then drawing his sword from its sheath he swung it around his head, the shiny, polished steel of the blade catching the glimmer of the sun.

"They are perched above us, looking down on the plain almost as a bird would. Are you sure they cannot see our men?" I asked.

"Lord Akiyama has taken great pains to hide everyone." The young guard looked at me severely, as if what I had said almost amounted to treason.

"Still, it is hard to guess from below what they can see from above," I argued, not caring to give in.

"That is why most of the mounted soldiers are hidden in that forest back there." The young samurai pointed to the place he meant.

"That is far from here," I could not help saying, for I realized it meant that we would be under attack almost as soon as the battle began, with no hope of immediate help.

"When the attack begins we are to retreat, leaving the archers and the foot soldiers who are hidden in the storehouse to fight. They will pursue us and we will draw them toward that point." Again, the young samurai used his head to point out the direction.

"And what about my men?" I asked in surprise, for I had not been told of this part of the strategy.

"They can fight or run, it does not matter. The more thorough their defeat, the more eager the enemy will be to pursue us. You have a horse — if I were you, I would retreat with us." The young samurai was eager to show himself my friend. "There will be no glory to catch here."

"No, only death," I muttered, but not loud enough for the young man to hear. At that moment Yoichi came up, carrying a bowl of tea for me. The old man was always finding ways of pleasing me, and if I smiled or gave the slightest nod as reward, he would act as if he had received a precious gift.

"Oh, I shall stay here," I said to the young commander. "These are my men and I will share whatever happens to them."

"But their duty is to die!" He shook his head. "It isn't important how long they hold out."

I shrugged my shoulders and did not answer. The thought that Lord Akiyama had placed me in a position from which I had but little chance of escaping made me wish to be alone to think the whole matter over. I looked up at the castle; it seemed so impregnable. Maybe they would not attack, and by tomorrow the plan would have to be abandoned. One could not hide the army forever.

"Who is in charge of the archers?" I asked.

"They are under my command." The young samurai straightened himself as he said this. "But there is an older soldier who will lead them."

"Has he been told of the plan?" I asked.

"No, it is not necessary. In a way, I think it will be better that it comes as a surprise to them, too, that we flee. It will be more likely to fool the enemy."

I nodded. Anger was rising within me. I understood that in a war people died — it was not a children's game with bamboo swords. It was the young man's attitude that irritated me, as if those poor farmers were but pawns in a game of chess. I walked away without showing my anger, for there was no point in that. The young man had courage enough, and had Lord Akiyama told him to stay and die, he would have done so.

Not far away from our position was a hillock, and I decided to climb it. The terrain was rough, not particularly good for a mounted charge. The sides of the hillock contained plenty of large rocks that would make it difficult for a horse to gain a foothold. Here we could hold out and have a chance, I thought to myself. As soon as the samurai spur their horses to flee, we should rush for this place. I nodded and smiled to myself. The plan was that we were to stay and die, but I had not been informed of this plan, so I was not disobeying it. I looked towards the rice hut where the twenty archers were hidden; with their help we might hold out long enough to save our lives.

The light was dim inside the hut. The men were sprawled on the floor, and as I entered they all looked up at me.

"Who is in command?" I asked.

An older man rose. He was wearing leather armor, and I guessed him to be some small farmer, a retainer of a none-too-rich samurai.

"Have you plenty of water?" I asked. "Or shall I have one of my men bring you some?"

"It would do no harm, if it is fresh." The older soldier smiled.

"If we have not been attacked by noon, I will see to it that you receive a ration of rice." I knew I was trying to buy their favor, but it was necessary if my plan was to succeed.

"That would not come amiss. We have had nothing but the most watery of gruel since the day before yesterday." The old soldier looked as pleased as if he were already tasting the rice I had promised.

"If the attack comes, I want you to follow my lead. The men on horseback may have to retreat, but we cannot." I lowered my voice a little for fear that someone might be listening. "There is a hillock nearby. If we gain that we may hold out long enough." I left it to the men's own imaginations to figure out what it was long enough for.

"That is a good plan." The old soldier looked overjoyed and the rest, thinking it wise to obey the "Master of Rice," grunted their agreement.

As soon as I was back among my own men, I ordered some of them to boil rice for the archers. I thought it best to feed them as early as possible, for I wanted them to trust me; after they had eaten my rice they were more liable to do so. The mounted samurai had their own fire where their servants were busy preparing their meals. I felt sure their servants had orders to flee at the first sign of an attack.

It was past midday. Both my men and the archers had received a plentiful meal when we first noticed movements within the castle that could mean the beginning of an attack. I told my men to look for their spears and went in search of the young samurai. He, too, had observed the activity within the walls and had ordered his men to stand by their beasts, ready to mount them. I noticed, as I had expected, that all their servants had already disappeared.

"It will come soon." The young man nodded as if he had ordered the attack personally. "If I were you, I would keep my horse near me. We will only stay until their soldiers have reached that point." The samurai pointed to a place halfway between the castle and our position.

At that moment the blowing of a conch shell could be heard, and a horseman who had been posted near the castle gate came galloping toward us, waving his hand to indicate that the gates to the castle had already been opened. The young officer told his men to mount and then turning to me said, "Order the archers to form a line in front of the hut and tell them to fight bravely."

I nodded in agreement, though I swore to myself that nothing as foolish as those words would come from my lips. Just as I turned to order the bowmen to come from the hut and take up position, the young samurai made a last appeal to me to join him and the others in their flight. I smiled, acknowledging that I had heard him, but did not reply.

As the archers came out from the hut, I saw the first of the mounted men leading the charge from the castle. Their banners fluttered as they galloped towards us. Pointing toward the hillock, I ordered my men of the Konidatai to seek refuge there, but I stayed with the bowmen.

"How many?" I asked the soldier who was in command of the archers. We were standing side by side.

"Two or three hundred."

The horsemen had split into two groups; one, consisting of perhaps a hundred, was heading toward us, their drawn swords flashing in the light of the noonday sun. When they reached the place that had been pointed out to me as the signal for our mounted men to flee, I ordered the bowmen to follow me and struck out towards the hillock. I had let my own horse wander off, hoping that it would be safe without a rider.

As we scrambled up the hillock, we could hear the shouts of the enemy attacking. Reaching the summit of the little hill, I ordered the bowmen to take up position and to shoot as soon as they judged the distance right for their arrows to be effective.

"Do not shoot before," I warned them. "Remember you have no more arrows than are in your quivers."

Drawing my sword, I stood in front of the men of the Konidatai, each of whom held a short spear in his hand. Our banners fluttered as gaily as those of our attackers. I looked back — our horsemen were fleeing.

Now is the time that we are supposed to die, I thought and grinned.

The first of the mounted men were now so close that we could plainly read the messages on their banners. At the foot of the hillock they reined in their horses, in doubt what to do next. Our arrows proved an answer to their question. One mounted man was badly hurt; another's horse shied as an arrow struck its flank. With a shout of anger, their leader spun his horse around, then, ordering his men to follow him, he galloped off in the direction of our fleeing horsemen — without knowing it, doing the bidding of Lord Akiyama.

The wounded man rode his horse toward the castle. He was badly hurt, and one of the younger men among the archers ran after him, a short spear in his hand. I watched as he caught up with the mounted samurai and thrust his spear from below. For a moment the warrior remained in the saddle, then he fell to the ground. The young bowman drew out the spear and thrust it into the dying man once more. I saw him stripping the man of his armor and helmet, but when he lifted the dead man's sword to sever head from body, I turned away.

"Kosuke is always lucky," the older soldier commented; he, too, had been watching. "We were lucky too. If we had stayed where we were, we would have been dead by now."

"But we would not have been important enough to lose our heads," I replied. The thought had occurred to me that this must have been the way my own father had lost his life. "I do not hold with this head cutting," I mumbled.

"It does not matter once you are dead. How else could we prove to our lords that we have fought bravely?" he asked, surprised at my words.

Just then the sound of a hundred conch shells being blown told us that the army of Lord Akiyama was no longer hiding. It saved me from answering the question, though I swore to myself that I would never collect such trophies.

A sortie that had started with high hopes was soon to end. As soon as the attackers realized that they had fallen into a trap, they tried to return to the castle. A few reached it, but most were cut down; perhaps less than twenty men returned. Some prisoners were taken and were kindly treated by Lord Akiyama. I could not help but feel sorry for the women within the castle who had watched their husbands' deaths.

The next day the Konidatai returned. We were busy unloading the horses and giving out rations of rice. Wada Kansuke was truly happy to see me, asking me several times to describe the fight and to explain in detail my plan that had saved the men. One would have thought that I had been the general in charge of a major battle, so proud he was of me.

I waited with some fear for the arrival of Lord Akiyama, for although I had not disobeyed any order, I had not behaved as I was supposed to. When he finally came he merely congratulated me and brought a suit of armor that he thought would fit me. It had been among the spoils of the battle. I thanked him, bowing deeply and keeping my head bent while he spoke to Wada Kansuke. The old samurai told him in detail of my exploits, and Lord Akiyama laughed. He was in high spirits and ordered us to give a double ration of rice and millet to everyone.

{ 22 }

Iwamura Is Ours

Our ruse had worked well; no sooner had the trap been set than the enemy had fallen into it. A few days later Lord Akiyama sent two of the prisoners as messengers to the castle. They were splendidly dressed in clothes my lord had given them and carried gifts as well as a letter. Although the contents of the missive were naturally a secret, a rumor soon spread that Lord Akiyama had offered to marry the widow of the lord of the castle and to keep all who were willing to serve him as retainers in the same positions they had held under Lord Toyama.

Wada Kansuke laughed when he heard this but did not deny that the hearsay might contain the truth. "They say that she is very beautiful, and to get a castle like Iwamura and a woman whom you need not feel ashamed of, either by lineage or by looks, would no doubt suit my lord."

"But if she is like her nephew, my lord had better sleep with his dirk under his pillow and ask her to taste his food first," I objected. "Besides, could she marry without her nephew's permission? After all, Nobunaga is head of the Oda clan."

"If she is as headstrong as most of that family, the very fact of having to ask would make her do it. I think Lord

Toyama was her third husband, so she will have some to compare Lord Akiyama with." Again, the samurai grinned.

"You would like him to marry her?" I asked, for I felt that Wada Kansuke believed the rumor because he approved of it.

"It would be well. There are those within the castle who are more friendly to Takeda Shingen than to Nobunaga. The Odas too are strangers here, more so than we from Kai. If the two of them should marry, we shall have conquered the castle more securely than we ever could by the sword." Kansuke looked down at the ground for a moment, then up at me. "Oda Nobunaga has decided upon her other husbands; maybe for once she would like to choose for herself. Toyama preferred his kept woman to her; he was afraid of her, or so I have been told. He was a sickly, weak man, not strong like our lord."

"Lord Akiyama is handsome," I said and nodded. "But she does not know that — I don't think she has ever seen him."

"She will ask her two young samurai to describe him, I am sure. I wonder if he has sent her a poem too?"

"Does Lord Akiyama write poetry?" I asked, a little surprised.

"No, but he can copy one with a fair hand, if someone else has written it." Wada Kansuke smiled as if recalling something that had taken place long ago. I could not help wondering if Kansuke had supplied my lord with poems when he had served him in the campaigns Lord Akiyama had fought when he was a young man.

"If the castle does not fall soon we shall have snow, and then those who burned the houses in the village will be sorry for their deeds." I had thought it unwise that we had destroyed so much of the village of Iwamura in our first attack; its more substantial buildings would have served us well in the winter months. And now I felt that it was even more foolish that we had burned the few hovels left before we had "retreated."

"It will fall." Wada Kansuke seemed confident. "They have hardly any food left — we got that news from the prisoners. Since we have promised to harm no-one and to let each retain his swords and his honor, there will be many among the samurai in favor of surrendering."

"But will they trust our word?" I could not help asking.

"Their empty stomachs will go a long way toward convincing them. It is well that Takeda Shingen has a reputation for keeping his word, whereas Oda is better known for his treachery. All this will be weighed when they take counsel, you may be sure of that."

For the next three days Lord Akiyama sent two prisoners each day to the castle bearing gifts and messages, yet he received no reply. Orders had been given to the archers who were stationed near the walls of the castle not to shoot unless they were attacked. The gifts sent to the castle contained nothing edible. I was told that Lord Akiyama had sent the Lady Toyama a set of brushes, an inkstone, and fine paper; considering that we had caught two of their messengers attempting to reach the nephew with letters from his aunt, the gift seemed to me ironic.

Most of the soldiers had but little to do; there was no longer any danger of a renewed attack from the castle, which left the bulk of the men restless. Hunting parties and an archery competition were arranged. My skill with bow and arrow was not such that I dared enter, but Yoshitoki had done so and I made a point of coming to watch. He had little chance of winning, for among the participants were some who were famous in all of Kai.

Lord Akiyama was among the spectators. It was a cold but clear day. The distance was fifty ken, at which I would have considered myself lucky to have hit the target at all. Yoshitoki was among the first to shoot. He did well enough not to disgrace himself and would be well among the upper half of the competitors. Stools had been put out for Lord Akiyama and the senior samurai. When Yoshitoki had finished he joined me; we stood among a group of young warriors not far away from the older samurai. I noticed that next to Lord Akiyama sat a young man whom I had never seen before. He wore an elegant hunting jacket of silk, with the mark of Lord Akiyama, an orange flower, on his sleeve.

"Who is he?" I asked Yoshitoki.

"Who?" Yoshitoki wrinkled his brow as if he did not understand whom I was talking about. I suspect that he knew perfectly well.

"The young man in the silk hunting jacket who is

sitting next to my lord and has a pale and sickly face," I said and turned to look at my friend.

"It is his son." Yoshitoki shrugged his shoulders. "He came a few days ago from Kofuchu. He is an adopted son."

I had heard of him but had never seen the young man. When I had stayed at the Akiyama mansion in Kofuchu he had been away at Takato Castle.

"He does not look well," I commented.

"They say that he has been very sick, but that he is better now." Yoshitoki looked at the young man whom we were discussing. "He looks as if he still carries some sickness within him."

In a moment of weakness I had told Yoshitoki of my dream that Lord Akiyama would adopt me; he had said nothing, only smiled. I thought now, as I watched my lord leaning towards his son and commenting upon the competition they were watching, that it had been a foolish fancy.

"I hope that you are wrong, and that he will truly get well." I wanted to make my friend understand that I had outgrown such childish dreams.

At that moment a samurai on horseback galloped up the field. Dismounting nearby he threw the reins to someone, then ran and knelt in front of Lord Akiyama. We could not hear what he said, he was too far away. It was obviously a message of some importance, for Lord Akiyama rose immediately and walked away, followed by his more important retainers.

By an unspoken mutual agreement, Yoshitoki and I walked away from the playing field and followed Lord

Akiyama. We were curious to find out what the message was. Lord Akiyama had moved his headquarters to a hillock from which a clear view of the castle and its gate was possible. Here a rude hut had been constructed that consisted of one large room. The top of the hillock was flat, and this small field had been divided by a cloth of dark blue that carried the orange flower of Lord Akiyama in its center. We did not dare go beyond the "wall" of cloth but waited impatiently with a group of samurai. We were told that a messenger from the castle had arrived, but that no-one knew as yet what news he had brought. I had noticed his horse, a magnificent beast, surely the best in the castle. A servant was holding its bridle at the foot of the little hill.

"They are going to surrender," I said. Yoshitoki shrugged his shoulders as if to say, "Who knows?"

I was right — Iwamura Castle was ours. One of the high-ranking samurai came out from behind the cloth screen; when he saw me he smiled and beckoned me to come. When I drew near and bowed, he bade me with a wave of his hand to follow him inside the hut.

"How much food can we spare?" Lord Akiyama frowned as if he were himself counting the kokus of rice, millet, and barley in our store.

"It depends upon how long we are to be here," I answered, a little confused, for after all, it was not an easy question to answer. "We have enough without fresh supplies for at least two months, keeping the rations as they are."

"Find Kasuke and tell him to come here. I want enough

rice brought to the castle so that no one within shall complain that an empty stomach has kept him awake this night. Tonight we guard the gate of Iwamura, and tomorrow we enter the castle. This is the agreement. No-one within the castle is to be treated as vanquished; all are to be treated as loyal retainers of Lord Takeda Shingen and myself." With a nod, Lord Akiyama dismissed me and I almost ran from the room, eager to fulfill his command.

{23}

In Search of Supplies

I think there is no castle in Japan situated better or more beautifully than the Castle of Iwamura. It is also known by the name "Castle of Mist." It received this name long ago when, during an attack by an enemy, the lord of the castle dropped the bones of a snake into a well. Immediately from the deep shaft a heavy mist arose that engulfed the whole mountain, throwing the attackers into such confusion that the castle was saved.

During the first few days I had but little time to admire the vast views from the castle walls or the buildings contained within them. On the first day we brought our scanty supplies into the empty storehouses of the castle. On the second, it was decided that we were to issue a measure of millet and barley to all those who had sought refuge in the castle. This was handed to them at the lower gate to ensure that they left. The task took a whole day and greatly depleted our stores. Lord Akiyama wanted to impress upon the people in the district that he had not come to destroy Iwamura Castle but to become its lord. The people took his grain and appeared thankful, but then it would have been very foolish of them to have behaved otherwise.

In the eleventh month of the year the weather turned bitterly cold. The horses and men of the Konidatai were still camped outside the castle, and they suffered much. Lord Akiyama decided to dismiss most of them and sent them back to the villages where they belonged. A small contingent was kept, for our supplies were running low and we were ordered to proceed to Iida Castle to obtain provisions. I was put in charge, and I chose the men carefully from among the youngest of the baggage train carriers. I had gotten permission for each man to lead two horses and not to carry any burdens himself; this meant that we could travel faster. At the last moment we were given an escort of twenty mounted samurai. It was never made clear who was in fact the commander — the elderly captain of the escort or me — and at times this made life very difficult for me.

Neither the captain nor any of the younger samurai had any desire to venture out of Iwamura Castle now that winter had come. They cursed their lot and held me and the poor peasants of the Konidatai responsible, not only for their being there but for the weather as well. They were constantly hurrying us, but as they were riding excellent horses and we were leading poor nags already worn out by carrying heavy packs, we could not always oblige them with the speed they desired. Though riding an excellent horse, I had to defend my poor barefoot carriers from being beaten. If only Yoshitoki had been in command of the samurai, how much easier the trip would have been. Oribe Minai, the captain, was a fool who thought himself wise. Quick to take offense if he thought himself slighted, he was at the same time afraid of making decisions. This was the worst combination possible in a commander. The trappings of power were all he desired, and toward him humility could not be overdone.

At Iida Castle we found that they had little rice to spare. I suggested that we should go to Takato Castle to see if we could obtain more there. Captain Oribe refused, saying that we had been ordered to go to Iida not to Takato. Finally, I took half of my men and proceeded to Takato Castle; the road was safe, and we needed no protection. At Takato I managed to obtain not rice but a load of millet. It was not of the best quality, but millet porridge tastes good if you are hungry enough.

Returning to Iida we met a lone samurai, a messenger on his way to Kofuchu from Takeda Shingen. He told us of the victory of the Takeda army at Mikatagahara and of how Tokugawa Ieyasu had had to flee for his life. When we met on that cold mountain pass it was a few days past the shortest day of the year. His description of the battle was not long-winded, as he was anxious to proceed to Takato Castle. I envied him his task, for he would certainly be rewarded and feasted wherever he went in Kai, as if it were he personally who had won the battle of Mikatagahara.

When we arrived at Iida there was a surprise in store for me. Captain Oribe had decided to return to Iwamura Castle without me and had taken along the twenty-five loads of rice that I had managed to obtain. I had left Yoichi in charge of the men of the Konidatai and I could not help wondering how he had fared with the quarrelsome captain. A servant in the castle gave me a message from him; the poor man was worried that I would take his departure for an act of disobedience. He need not have feared, because I realized that he could not have done other than to obey the old samurai.

I did not miss the captain, although the territory through which we had to travel was one that warranted an escort. However, this did not worry me; I was only worried that he would arrive before me with twenty-five loads of rice and a tale of my insubordination. If I had at least been able to obtain rice or barley to excuse my journey to Takato Castle, all would have been well. We stayed at Iida for two days to rest the horses, then we set out for Iwamura, hauling our load of moldy millet.

I almost wished that we would be attacked by bandits or some of Oda Nobunaga's forces; that would have made it difficult for Captain Oribe to defend his decision to abandon us. Nothing but the usual calamities happened — a horse falling and breaking its leg, another suddenly going lame — but these were matters that I was used to handling. Decisions that a few months before would have caused me great concern I now made at a moment's notice.

As soon as we arrived at Iwamura Castle, I hastened to find Wada Kansuke. I told him what had happened and asked his advice. He smiled at my description of Captain Oribe; he knew him well. He also knew that the captain had been to see Lord Akiyama. As soon as I had unloaded the millet, he counseled me to seek an audience with my lord. I was to be frank, he advised, but should not blame Oribe Minai too much. After all, he thought,

I had been successful, and my twenty-five loads of millet were needed.

When I had dismissed my men and had made certain that they were to be fed and housed, I hastened to the main building. There I saw a high-ranking samurai who was close to Lord Akiyama and asked him to enquire whether my master would see me. I was told that I might come the following morning, when Lord Akiyama received anyone who had a complaint or desired a favor. I felt that this was a deliberate snub. Wada Kansuke consoled me and told me not to worry, but I did not sleep well that night despite my tiredness after the long journey.

I arrived punctually next morning, but others who came much later were admitted before me. The old samurai who attended those seeking an audience was named Zakoji. His mode of behavior was extremely formal; I could not help feeling that he had been brought up in a palace. I later found out that he had been born and had spent his childhood in Kyoto, where his father had served the Emperor. I waited patiently, showing neither anger nor annoyance when others were admitted before me.

At last my turn came, for there was no-one left to be given preference over me. I was admitted to a small room that had beautifully painted sliding doors. I could not keep my eyes away from one that portrayed a giant peacock. In the center of the room sat Lord Akiyama; on a small wooden table beside him rested his swords. He was dressed more splendidly than I had ever seen him before, in a blue silk kimono. I knelt in front of him and bent my head low, but did not speak. I waited and at last he spoke; I tried to guess from the tone of voice if he was angry with me.

"You had no orders to go to Takato Castle." It was phrased almost as a question, and for that reason I dared answer as I did.

"I had been ordered to get supplies enough for fifty horses to carry. At Iida I found only enough for twenty-five. If I had returned with only half the amount of supplies I had been commanded to get, then I would indeed have disobeyed my master."

"And was there rice to be got at Takato?" Lord Akiyama asked.

"No rice, my lord," I answered, looking up at him. "The commander of the castle spared me loads of millet for your sake. He was most pleased at your victory and bade me tell you so. He was sorry that he had little rice, but he gave me one koku-weight of it for your table."

"That was most kind, for I am sure that he had sent all that he could spare to Lord Takeda. What did he think of the news of Lord Takeda's victory?" Lord Akiyama's voice was pleasant and frank, as if he were talking to an equal.

"He had not heard, sir. We met the messenger from Lord Takeda on our return journey to Iida. I am sure it must have pleased him greatly — he had only a few soldiers in his castle."

"Did the messenger tell you of Lord Takeda Shingen's

health?" Lord Akiyama lowered his voice as if he did not want to be overheard asking that question.

"No, my lord." I shook my head. "We met in a mountain pass. It was very cold; he was shivering and his teeth were chattering from the icy weather." I could not help smiling a little as I recalled the messenger. "I think he was more interested in safeguarding his own health inside Takato Castle than in telling me of Lord Takeda's."

"I have had further news that he is not well. But I do not want this spread about as common gossip. If you should hear anyone passing on such rumors, note the man and tell me."

"I shall, my lord." I bowed my head to indicate that I had heard and would obey.

"As for the millet, we are pleased to have it." Lord Akiyama paused for a moment. "You seem better fitted to command alone than to serve under others. . . ." Lord Akiyama smiled a little. "But I suppose it would ill suit me to call that a fault. Here!" Lord Akiyama had taken a gold coin from a purse and held it out to me. I took it from his hand and bowed my head to the ground. Everyone knew that Lord Akiyama did not like to be second in command, and so he seldom served under others. Lord Takeda Shingen acknowledged this — that was why my lord had been sent against Iwamura Castle instead of remaining with the main forces that had fought at Mikatagahara.

"I thank you, my lord." I rose and walked backward from the room. Once outside I smiled; my audience had gone well. I turned towards the old samurai in order to thank him and pay my respect. To my surprise, a young woman was standing beside him. She was not a servant; she was dressed in a silk kimono of such elegance as I had never seen before, with sleeves so wide that they almost reached the floor. Her face was pale, like the color of the full moon when it has reached the zenith of the sky. I am afraid I stared like a foolish peasant or a priest who has seen the living Buddha descend from the skies.

"My daughter," the old samurai grumbled, ill-pleased with the meeting. Then, unnecessarily, he explained why she was there, telling me that she had come with a message from Lady Toyama.

I looked down quickly and then bowed very deeply to Lord Zakoji and his beautiful daughter. I felt my cheeks blushing but, although I felt ashamed of having stared, as I left the room I managed out of the corner of my eye to have yet another glance at the moon girl in the silk kimono.

{24}

Aki-hime

To write about the first time that love enters your life is not easy, for it is often coupled with many a foolish act that leaves a bittersweet taste. I could not wait, but searched out a servant of Captain Zakoji as soon as I had left Lord Akiyama. The servant, an older man, could scarcely hide his smile when I eagerly demanded to know the name of his master's daughter.

"Which one?" he asked. "He has several, you know."

"I think she must be a little younger than myself, sixteen summers, I would guess."

"It must be Aki-hime you mean. She will be sixteen this year. The other daughters are all older . . . and married." The old man's lips twisted a little from suppressed laughter.

"And she . . . is she betrothed?" The question was asked as if my life depended upon its answer. Though I knew I was making a fool of myself, I did not mind.

"She was, but he is dead. She was to have been married this coming summer." The old servant added, a little maliciously, "He was a great lord in Mino country and had a great estate just like my master."

But he is dead, I thought, and never had the news of another man's death brought me greater pleasure. Yet I realized at that moment that there would be other samurai with large estates eager to ask for Aki-hime in marriage. As I walked back to my own quarters I said her name over and over again "Aki . . . Aki" and found it the loveliest girl's name that I had ever heard.

That night I had great difficulty in falling asleep; one plan more absurd than the next formed in my mind. My wealth was quickly counted: some clothes, a sword, a dagger, a suit of armor, and a helmet — no great estate to marry on. As I lay restless long past the hour of the rat, I realized that I was, in truth, no better than a ronin, a samurai in the great marketplace of Japan with a sword for sale. If I were wise I would search for the daughter of some wealthy farmer who might be pleased at gaining a two-sword man as a son-in-law and might slip him some silver or gold for the favor of marrying his daughter. Or, I should marry an older woman, or one whose face or character made it difficult for her to find a suitor. But Lord Zakoji's daughter was beautiful and her father was rich, they said, and well-connected. I would not even be able to get anyone to approach him and make so foolish a proposal as to suggest me as his son-in-law. No, it was impossible even to think about, and yet I did. If Lord Akiyama would speak for me, I thought — and then imagined my lord rewarding me with some estate somewhere that would suddenly make me a wealthy man. Fondling that daydream in my mind, I fell asleep.

Morning found me more clear-headed. I even argued that I had seen the girl but for a fleeting moment and that she might not be so desirable after all. All that I learned about Lord Zakoji made the gulf between me and the girl's father wider and deeper. He was indeed a wealthy samurai who could lay claim to respect. He had served the lord of the castle as Master of the Storehouse, in charge of collecting the taxes of the district. This made me search out Wada Kansuke, for I felt sure that the old samurai would know something about him.

"He was one of those in favor of surrendering the castle, that I know," he answered when I asked him what kind of man the captain was.

"Because he feared for his life?" I asked.

"I think he had little love for Lord Toyama and even less for Oda Nobunaga. No, I don't think it was fear of death. . . . At one time he served Lord Takeda Shingen, or at least supported him. He is a man who is his own master. They say that he is a master of calligraphy. I think he paints too. . . . But why are you so eager to know about him?" The leader of the Konidatai looked at me inquisitively.

"I am just curious," I answered lamely and then, to make my enquiry more plausible, I added, "He was the one who served Lord Akiyama when I asked and was permitted to see him. Either he or Lord Akiyama had me wait while ordinary archers and foot soldiers got preference."

"And did you show your annoyance at this?" Kansuke smiled.

"No, I acted as though I did not notice and was as respectful to the captain as if he had admitted me before anyone else."

"That was wise. They were testing you to see if you

had grown in judgment as well as in height." Wada Kansuke laughed.

A few days later I was told that I had been detailed to form part of a guard to accompany a high-ranking officer to Nagashino Castle. I was pleased, for it was an honor — none of the guards had been chosen from the lower-ranking samurai. I was even more pleased when I found that my friend Yoshitoki had also been picked. We were to be fifty men; Lord Akiyama had selected us from among the highest-born and from those who would make the most pleasing appearance. I think that Yoshitoki and I had been selected because of our ability on horseback. The officer in charge was Lord Akiyama's flag carrier. He was an imposing man, very strong, and taller than most of us. I was given new armor and I wore the helmet I had won. Our horses were the very best from Lord Akiyama's stable. Lord Takeda Shingen was at Nagashino Castle; his army was quartered there. We were not only to guard the envoy, our duty was also to reflect the glory of our master and commander, Lord Akiyama.

Each samurai was to take one servant and a supply of food with him. I chose Yoichi, who was loyal and very attached to me; he was the oldest among the servants as I was the youngest of the samurai. He was also a mere peasant, whereas most of the other servants had been brought up in the houses of their masters. I did not care, for I knew him to be much cleverer than all the others, though much fun was made of my orderly.

I had given little thought to whom we would be guarding, as I considered it no concern of mine. The night before we were to leave Yoshitoki came to visit me and to ask if I was ready and had everything that I needed. I told him that I had been given an almost new suit of armor laced with the colors of Lord Akiyama and that I would be more splendidly dressed than ever before in my life. This made him laugh.

He declared, "A suitor could not be too elegantly clothed."

"A suitor?" I asked, thinking of the "moon princess."

"Lord Akiyama wants to marry Lady Toyama, and he is sending Lord Zakoji to ask Lord Takeda Shingen's permission. So we are fifty suitors all dressed for the part . . ."

"Lord Zakoji," I whispered. This was a surprise. "And what about Lady Toyama, is she willing?" I asked.

"I haven't asked her myself," Yoshitoki grinned. "But then the ladies' quarters are fiercely guarded here."

"Have you ever seen her?" I demanded.

"Once, but at a distance. She was surrounded by her maids. Lord Zakoji's daughter was among them; they say she is beautiful."

"She is." I felt my face grow red and wished I had said nothing. "I saw her once; she had come with a message for Lord Akiyama from her mistress."

Such was Yoshitoki's sensitivity that he did not ask any of the questions I am sure he would have liked to. Instead, he changed the subject to ask me what horse I would ride the following day.

"I would have preferred to ride my usual mare, but her color is wrong. We are to be mounted on horses that would not disgrace the greatest lords of Japan. Lord Akiyama wants the coat of each to match the others; all are to be as near to black as can be found."

"We are suitors!" Yoshitoki laughed as he repeated his joke, and then added more seriously, "But it is a wise marriage, for as long as Lady Toyama exists, our lord is not the true ruler of Iwamura Castle. Once she has become Lady Akiyama he can govern here as if he were born to it."

"Do you think she loves him?" I asked.

Yoshitoki slapped his thigh. "Lord Toyama was her third husband, I think. Three times she has been married for the convenience of her nephew, Oda Nobunaga. This time she has made her own choice, but whether it is for love or for some other reason I cannot tell."

Somehow I hoped that it was for love. I was thinking of Lord Zakoji's daughter, trying to recall the features of her face.

{25}

Lord Takeda Shingen

We made a splendid sight as we left Iwamura Castle. Lord Akiyama watched us with a retinue of high-ranking samurai as we trotted past. He held a fan in his hand and acknowledged our homage by lifting it. He was clad in silk, and I could not help thinking, Oh, it must be love — look how careful he has become of his dress.

The journey itself was uneventful; the weather was cold but clear, and we had no rain. During the whole trip I never saw Lord Zakoji speak to anyone. He rode in complete silence with his personal servant beside him; in front of him rode twenty-five of the samurai of his escort and another twenty-five followed him. Yoshitoki and I were among the last. Our servants followed us at a proper distance so that they did not interfere with our dignity. Whenever we met peasants on our way, they would fall on their knees, but the women, especially the young girls, would just stand and stare. If they were pretty, the young samurai would sit even straighter in their saddles.

Most of Lord Shingen's army was still quartered near Noda Castle, but there must have been at least ten thousand soldiers camped in and near Nagashino Castle. The castle itself is not so impressive, although it is good for defense. The camps of the army encompassed a great territory around the castle, and as we rode through we attracted the attention of everyone. Considering that this was an army that had just won a great victory and only a few days before had captured the castle of Noda, a strangely subdued, unhappy mood seemed to prevail. Several old friends from Kofuchu came to greet us, but even they seemed out of sorts. Finally we were told that Takeda Shingen lay ill in the castle, and that he was so weak that he could not stand up. His belly was swollen like that of a woman about to give birth. Two Buddhist priests who were wise in matters of medicine had given little hope for his life.

"Where is Lord Katsuyori?" one of us asked.

"He is here." It was more the tone of the voice than what was said that told me the speaker's opinion of Katsuyori: he will never become the leader his father is, he will never receive that unquestioning loyalty from his soldiers that all great warlords must have in order to succeed. It struck me that even if his father should die, Katsuyori would remain the Wakatono, the son of the lord, rather than becoming the lord himself.

Conditions were very rough. Lord Zakoji was housed in the castle itself, but we were lucky to be given a barn to shelter in. We were cold, and wished ourselves back in Iwamura.

It was said that the news of Lord Akiyama's intended marriage had brought a smile to Lord Takeda Shingen's face for the first time in weeks. He had presented Lord Zakoji with a heavy purse of Kofu gold to be taken to Lord Akiyama as a wedding present. We were not told any of this by Lord Zakoji, who held himself as aloof as ever, but by others who stood near to Lord Takeda and were not so proud that they would not talk to us.

The day before we were to leave on our return journey, I was called to the castle as Lord Zakoji wished to speak to me. On my way there I speculated as to what possible reason he could have for wishing to see me.

I did not know in what manner I should greet him, but feeling certain that any form of familiarity would be a mistake, I merely kneeled at the very entrance to the room and said, "You have sent for me, my lord."

"Come closer!" The old samurai beckoned with his hand as he pushed a cushion a little in my direction as an indication that I might sit down. I chose to kneel rather than sit on the cushion, which made the old man smile.

"I can no longer hear as well as I could in my youth when I could hear the grass grow and the footsteps of a maiden creeping home from a meeting with her lover." The old samurai laughed. "Now you know my secret, young man."

"I am sorry, my lord," I said and then paused because I did not know what else to say. Finally I added, "It must be a great discomfort."

"Discomfort . . ." Lord Zakoji paused as if he were tasting my word. He seemed almost to have swallowed it as he finally said, "Yes, that is very good, young man. Discomfort, that is exactly what deafness causes. It is not the fact that you cannot hear what others say that annoys you — for few people have anything of importance to say. No, it is the fact that it interferes with your dignity. . . . A wise man can appear a fool to the fools of this world because of his deafness."

"I do not think that anyone would dare to think of you in that manner," I protested. Now I understood the reason for Lord Zakoji's silence during the journey.

"It should not matter to me. It is vanity to be annoyed when fools laugh at you. When one reaches my age, one should only be concerned with finding the Way, the road that leads to Buddha."

I nodded, at the same time wondering if I would ever live to be so old that I would shed all worldly desires.

"Lord Takeda wishes to see you, that is why I sent for you." Lord Zakoji looked at me for a moment as if he wondered why Lord Takeda should care to see me. "It seems that you have met my lord once before," he added with a smile.

"It was a long time ago." I felt my face flush with pleasure. "I am surprised that my lord remembered."

"Lord Akiyama reminded him in a letter, in which he also told him that you killed Hanagata Minbu."

"I only wounded him," I protested. "He committed seppuku afterward."

"And were you his kaishaku-nin?"

"No! No!" I answered vehemently, for the thought of cutting off another man's head repulsed me. "Wada Kansuke was his kaishaku-nin," I said.

The old samurai nodded in approval, then he rose and told me to follow him.

Yes, that was right, I thought, Wada Kansuke had been

his friend and was of the same age. . . . If I had been his kaishaku-nin it would have been wrong, not the decent and dignified act of a friend.

The largest room in the castle was used by Lord Takeda. He was seated by a brazier and wore a padded coat, but I think he was still cold, as if the warmth of life had partly left him. I kneeled in front of him and bowed my head so low that my forehead touched the floor. For a moment he said nothing, merely contemplated me as if he were guessing my weight. Just as his silence became almost unbearable, he said, "Lord Akiyama has written about you."

I bowed but said nothing.

"He has been pleased with you, and he is not easy to please." This time when Lord Takeda ceased speaking, I spoke.

"I am honored to serve Lord Akiyama, and pleased that he is satisfied with me."

"Haruchika." Lord Takeda smiled as he pronounced his own pet name for Lord Akiyama. "Haruchika is a great soldier, the best of all my generals." Lord Takeda Shingen paused as he recalled all the campaigns he had fought. "How did you kill Hanagata Minbu?"

"I did not kill him, sir, I only wounded him. It was a fight fought on horseback on a very narrow trail. It was more my luck than experience or skill, I am sure."

"He was my enemy." Lord Takeda smiled as if he found that amusing. "I have had many enemies, but now there is only one left that matters. . . . And that one you cannot fight." Lord Takeda looked down at his own swollen body and then into space as if he could see the road to the west, the road to death, in front of him. For a long time the great warlord sat silent, then he groped inside the sleeve of his padded coat and brought out a gold coin. "Here!" he said. "For Minbu's head." I crawled forward and took the coin from his hand, which was white and swollen so that I could see the veins. "Serve Haruchika to the end," he admonished.

"I shall, my lord," I answered and suddenly the thought came to me — once Lord Takeda was dead, how long would it take before Lord Akiyama should fall too?

"To the end. . . ." Lord Takeda repeated his words and then, taking up his famous iron war-fan, he made a movement with it, indicating my dismissal.

Lord Zakoji had been kneeling at the entrance to the room, and now he left with me. As we went outside he said, "He seemed better today."

I looked at him in surprise, for, to me, Lord Takeda had looked so sick that I thought there was no hope for him.

"He must get well soon," Lord Zakoji mumbled.

"What will happen if he should die?" I asked.

"Everything will be over. The Wakatono is no match for Oda Nobunaga. Lord Takeda must not die." The last words were spoken in a tone that allowed for no argument. He had not referred to Katsuyori by name but had used his title, Wakatono, and this showed his lack of faith in him. Lord Zakoji invited me to his room, where tea was served. He was most friendly, but I guessed that he was shy by nature and I felt deeply honored by his attention to me. Once, in passing, he mentioned his daughter, Aki-hime, as he told me that his wife was dead. To hear her name on her father's lips brought pleasure to me.

⟨26⟩

A Poem for Aki-hime

On our way back to Iwamura I had several conversations with Lord Zakoji. He was well read, not only in the Buddhist sages but in literature too. He declared that he never wrote poetry because he had too great a respect for those who wrote well to insult them by making clumsy imitations. I did not believe him but felt certain that in secret drawers of his writing desk at home there would be some poems, and that they would be neither badly composed nor badly written, for he was famous for his calligraphy. He opened to me a world that was so different from the rough and all too ready world of the young samurai, where physical fitness counts for everything. I liked his gentle ways, the little rituals that formed part of his life; even during our journey he drank his tea out of exquisite cups that his servant carried in a little wooden box. His dainty, almost feminine, habits were not laughed at, for Lord Zakoji sat well in his saddle and was known as one of the most accomplished swordsmen in Japan. He once let me hold one of his swords, a great honor; it was heavier than most, and the hilt was inlaid with gold. It had been made by a great master of the art, a famous sword maker of Kyoto. I think Lord Zakoji owned nothing that was not valuable—even his combs were not wooden, like mine, but were made of tortoiseshell, their tops framed in silver.

Once we were back in Iwamura Castle I was eager to continue my friendship with Lord Zakoji, but many weeks passed before I saw him again. Lady Toyama became the wife of Lord Akiyama in a simple ceremony held in the little Hachiman shrine in the castle. No feast was held and only a few gifts were given to the highest-ranking samurai.

I had confessed to my friend Yoshitoki my feelings for Lord Zakoji's daughter. He made fun of me good-naturedly, and I felt sure he thought my case too hopeless, my rank much too low for such aspirations. The result was that I dared not speak to anyone else about it. No, that is not quite true — I had spoken to my servant, Yoichi. He was so loyal that he thought no woman in Japan too highly placed for me, and it was through him that I made contact with Aki. The samurai and the lords are like trees, and their servants are like the roots. The trees stand apart from each other; their branches may not even touch, although their roots are entangled.

We had not been back very long before Yoshitoki was detailed to form part of an escort that was to take a boy held hostage at Iwamura Castle to Kofuchu. The eight-year-old boy was called Gobo; he was the fifth and youngest son of Oda Nobunaga. He was a likable little fellow. I hoped they would treat him well at Tsutsujigasaki Castle. I rode along part of the way the first day. The boy was mounted on a small horse; he was already an accomplished rider. As we parted I rather envied my friend his commission, for I was back in the stores of the castle, working with Wada Kansuke.

I took my time riding back. It was a lovely day and soon the cherry blossom would be out in Kofuchu. For no reason at all, my thoughts turned to Lord Takeda. We had not heard any news for weeks, and I felt certain that before the new leaves formed on the trees, he would be dead. Now that his soul was ready to depart on that last journey it makes without the body, did he think of his son whom he had condemned to death? I shook my head and kicked my horse into a gallop to get rid of such thoughts.

I had a tiny room of my own in one of the lesser buildings of the castle. Yoichi made my food, and, although he was no great cook, he was an accomplished fisherman, and I would often have trout or some other fish for my supper. That particular evening the fish was large and I complimented him on it. Kneeling beside my little table, he bobbed his head up and down, pleased by my compliments.

"Master," he said, "I have talked to someone who serves Lord Zakoji. He is a servant of no importance or he would not have deigned to talk to me, but he does know one of the serving women and would be willing, through her, to pass a message to the high-born young lady."

I laughed, but turned the idea over in my mind. I could write a letter or — better — a poem and send it to her. . . . I did not feel sure that I could write anything worthy of her. Nevertheless, no sooner had I eaten than I brought out my inkstone, brush, and paper. I made several attempts before I was satisfied, then I wrote it out carefully, making my letters at least distinct if not beautiful.

The buds on the plum tree
Contain the hope of spring.
Born in winter and alone,
I long to see them unfurled.

I gave the poem to Yoichi that very evening. As soon as it was out of my hand, I decided it was a very poor poem. "Born in winter and alone" made me seem pathetic, and yet it was true. Or was it? True, I had no parents to love me, no mother to spoil me, but others had been kind. Would she not feel contempt rather than love, and did I not deserve it for having written so foolish a poem? All that night such thoughts kept me from sleeping and it was not until the light of dawn had begun to paint the mountains that I fell asleep.

The next day a rider appeared with a message for Lord Akiyama, bidding him to come to Komaba. Lord Takeda Shingen was resting in a temple there on his way back to Kofuchu. The messenger looked so stern that no-one dared approach him, but the expression on his face was an ill omen for our future.

At noon, Yoichi gave me a folded letter. It was tied with a ribbon in which was stuck a sprig from a plum tree. Hastily I tucked it in my sleeve and ran to my room. Once I had closed the sliding door behind me and had taken out the letter, I was so afraid of untying the ribbon that I sat with the letter in my hand for a long time before undoing it. On a paper faintly tinged with pink, the color of plum blossom, she had written three lines.

The bud on the plum tree fears to unfurl.
It knows that the splendor of its petals
Will fall to earth for others to tread on.

"Aki," I whispered to myself, not adding the "hime," which is just a title of honor given to a high-born maid. Then I smiled. I felt that I already knew the girl and that I could win her. Now to write a poem that would answer hers. I brought out my tools for writing, but the paper I had was of very poor quality and I felt ashamed of using it. I would have to get some that was better — but first I would have to compose the poem. I set to work immediately, forgetting that I had an appointment with Wada Kansuke. I finally decided on three lines, the same length as hers.

When the storm comes it will break the boughs
And scatter the petals of the flowers wide.
I shall gather them and keep them in my sleeve.

The storm I referred to I did not take seriously, yet if Lord Takeda Shingen should die it would come. Would I be able to protect her? I was very young and gave little thought to what would happen tomorrow. What was more important was to find paper of fine enough quality to serve for my message. I ran to Wada Kansuke, only remembering as I entered the storehouse that I was supposed to have been there some time ago. Some peasants were hauling sacks of millet around, opening them for his inspection, so I did not like to ask about the paper. Not until the workmen had left and we were alone did I dare approach him. At first he looked a little annoyed, guessing almost immediately my reason for asking for the paper. Suddenly he smiled and demanded to know my age.

"I shall be twenty soon, I think." I blushed for I felt it shameful that I did not know the day or month when I was born, I had been so young when my parents died. "I am not sure," I said. "I may be only nineteen." I laughed to hide my embarrassment.

"You are lucky, you can choose your own dates for the soothsayers to make a horoscope from." Wada Kansuke grinned.

"Has Lord Akiyama left?" I asked.

"He left before the foam on the messenger's horse had dried. I saw him leave; his face was pale like a winter moon."

"If Lord Takeda Shingen should die, Lord Katsuyori will be our ruler," I said.

Wada Kansuke just shrugged his shoulders, and then, as if he could not bear to talk about it anymore, he asked me to come to his room. Once there, he searched long until he found two sheets of very fine paper. He handed them to me, pointing out with a smile that they were large enough to be cut in two. He did not ask why I wanted the paper, and I could not help wondering if he knew to whom I was writing. I hurried back to my room and wrote out my poem, then I gave it to Yoichi to deliver. The next day I waited all day long, expecting a reply, but none came.

The following day Lord Akiyama returned. I watched him as he dismounted and entered the castle. To my surprise, I noticed Lord Zakoji among the retinue. Then I understood why I had received no reply to my poem: Aki had not thought it seemly to answer while her father was away. The next day Yoichi brought me her reply, written on plain white paper:

The frost that comes out of season
Will kill the budding flower.
Spring, dressed in winter's cloth,
Leaves no fruit for summer ripeness.

{27}

Lord Zakoji's Proposal

Now followed a strange time! Almost all of us knew that Lord Takeda Shingen was no more, yet no-one admitted that he had died. Rumors were spread that he had returned to Kofuchu and was well. These no-one believed, yet no-one dared say they were untrue. It had been Lord Shingen's wish that his death be kept secret in order to keep his opponents from invading his lands. On each border of our province was an enemy: to the north, Uesugi Kenshin, whom Lord Shingen had fought five times; to the east, Hojo Ujimasa, a very doubtful friend; to the south and to the west, the two great enemies of the Takedas — Tokugawa Ieyasu and, the most ruthless of all the warlords of Japan, Oda Nobunaga. So many tigers waiting to pounce on Kai!

By the beginning of summer it had become impossible to keep the secret of Lord Shingen's death any longer. Lord Akiyama left for Kofuchu, where a council was to be held to which all the higher-ranking officers had been invited.

A few days before this I received an invitation to come to Lord Zakoji's room. I had not spoken to him since our return to Iwamura Castle, and I was frightened that the exchange of letters between his daughter and myself had come to his attention. The letters had been innocent enough, but, even so, it was not correct for me to write without having obtained her father's permission.

It was with some fear that I entered the room. Lord Zakoji did not seem angry and invited me kindly to sit down and make myself comfortable, as if he were receiving not a young man of little account, but a friend. At first he spoke of that which occupied all our minds, as freely as if I, too, were in Lord Akiyama's confidence. I was careful of what I said in reply, for I understood that the lords, the generals of the Takeda army, had divided into two groups, one of which supported Katsuyori. These were mostly those who hailed from Suwa province and the younger men. The other group wished Katsuyori's infant son to become the ruler and, until he came of age, the territory to be ruled by a council, with Takeda Katsuyori as a vice-ruler who would have to obey the decisions of the council. This group consisted of the older and more experienced of the generals. I sympathized with them but, at the same time, understood how Katsuyori must feel being set aside in favor of his son. From Lord Zakoji I understood that our master, Lord Akiyama, belonged to the second group. The meeting that was to be held in Tsutsujigasaki Castle in Kofuchu would decide who was to rule Kai. Suddenly Lord Zakoji grew silent as we heard the rustle of someone moving beyond the door. Slowly the door slid open, revealing a young girl — it was Aki-hime. She brought in a small table with tea and some rice cakes, which she placed in front of me, then she returned to bring another table, handed to her by her maid, which she put in front of her father.

"My clumsy and ugly daughter," Lord Zakoji said with a smile that belied what he had said. Aki blushed and the faint pinkness that colored her white cheeks was the tinge of a petal of plum blossom. She bowed to me and to her father and then left the room. With a wave of his hand, Lord Zakoji motioned me to partake of the fare. Almost as embarrassed as poor Aki, I bit into the rice cake, feeling sure that her father knew all about my letters.

"I have been unworthy of the happiness of having a son." Lord Zakoji looked at his teacup. "It has occurred to me that some day I may find someone who would not mind the plainness of my daughter nor my undistinguished name, so that my youngest daughter's husband would become my son."

I could not speak; so great was the honor shown me by this hint that Lord Zakoji wished me to bear his family name that I became tongue-tied. The expression on my face must have been plain to read, as Lord Zakoji held up his hand to tell me to remain silent.

"My daughter is young and the times we live in so uncertain that I have not yet decided when I should search for such a young man or if he can be found. My name may be more of a burden than a marriage gift worth taking."

"I am sure that there is many a young man who would think it a great honor to exchange his name for yours,"

I managed to say. My hand shook as I lifted the teacup to my lips.

"Both my sons-in-law have strong links to their own families, therefore I thought that for my youngest daughter I would choose someone who might be more easily absorbed into mine . . . Someone who has neither father nor mother . . ." For a moment the old samurai allowed a smile to light his face, then he said, "But let some time pass, let us see what happens."

I do not remember what else was said that afternoon. I was much too overwhelmed by what had happened. I rushed to my room and tried to compose a poem that would describe my good fortune. But nothing that I wrote pleased me. It was as if my very happiness had made me dumb. Lord Zakoji's statement that he would wait because of the uncertainty of our times before adopting some young man as his son made it impossible for me to tell any of my friends of my good luck.

Lord Zakoji left with Lord Akiyama, as did most of the higher-ranking samurai. I wrote several poems and letters to Aki while her father was away and, as before, she did not answer. I did not mind this, for, through my servant, I learned that she had confessed to her maid that she cared for me. Yoichi had become dear to me, for I could talk to him about my feelings and he would approve of every high-flown plan of mine. Suddenly I took an even greater interest in my work. I was still Wada Kansuke's assistant, and we were concerned with tax gathering and supplies. Once I became Lord Zakoji's son, would not that be the very work that I would have at least to supervise, if not carry out? Already I thought of myself as a young lord.

It was midsummer before Lord Akiyama returned from Kofuchu. We guessed immediately from the stern expression on his face that it had not gone well for his side. A council of older officers had been formed, but they could only give advice, not orders. Katsuyori was now our Oyakata-sama, Lord of Kai. As for Lord Shingen's advice that after his death the Takeda armies should not fight outside their own territory, no-one believed it would be followed by the son. What the older samurai feared most of all was that Katsuyori would start an attack upon his enemies before he was prepared for it.

The return of Lord Akiyama and Aki's father meant that I again received replies to my letters and poems. I had asked one of Lord Akiyama's servants to purchase paper for me in Kofuchu, and now I had an ample supply to disfigure with my poems.

{28}

The Hunting Party

In the fall of that year we heard that Nagashino Castle had been taken by Tokugawa Ieyasu. Lord Katsuyori had sent troops to aid the garrison, but they had arrived too late and had been too few to dare to attack the Tokugawa army. Lord Zakoji told me that Lord Akiyama was afraid that Katsuyori-sama would attack his enemies too soon. The fall of Nagashino was a pinprick, not a wound, and should be treated as such. No attempt to recapture the castle should be made. Lord Zakoji wanted Lord Katsuyori to make peace with Oda and Tokugawa and to give up the thought of being ruler of Japan, leaving such dreams to others. But dreams are strong as iron. They say that a wild horse can be tied with a spider's web; certain it is that a man can be tied by a dream.

That winter, Lord Zakoji continued to be friendly to me but, although he knew that I considered myself a suitor for his daughter, he did not mention again the idea of adopting me. I once asked Wada Kansuke if he would consider acting as my go-between. He asked, with a smile, where I would keep my wife, for he thought my room hardly large enough to make a home for a family. When he saw how downcast I looked, he took pity on me and tried to comfort me by saying that he would speak to Lord Akiyama when he judged the moment opportune.

Lord Zakoji's friendship was too valuable to lose by some hasty act; the old samurai was a stickler for form, and any sign of impropriety would have upset him.

"It is always difficult to see your last child married and becoming the wife or husband of some stranger. It will make him an old man, too, don't you see?" Kansuke pointed a finger at me. "Soon after you are married and he has adopted you, you will wish to be the master of his estate, and he will have to be satisfied with playing with his grandchildren and sitting under a cherry tree."

I could not help laughing, for there was truth in what he had said. I was ambitious, ever dreaming of rising above the station I occupied. Power and fame — yes, I wanted both as much as did Takeda Katsuyori.

Not until spring did Lord Zakoji mention the subject again, and then it was not in a manner that made me more hopeful. He had invited me to his room, and tea was served by Aki. This time neither she nor I blushed when we saw each other. As she left she smiled shyly. I felt my heart beating faster, and I swore to myself that she would be my wife.

What her father had to say did not encourage any such thought, for the old samurai talked long and gloomily about the cherry blossom that we praise because it is so short-lived.

"The life of man is like the morning dew, which can bestow pearls on the grass; but the sun of noon makes them disappear," he said. "All our ambitions and hopes are but vanity, which keep us from the Way."

"If we have not ambitions to form our hopes when we

are young, sir, would there be any palaces or even temples to worship in?" I asked, while I thought, To the old, life is, in truth, short, and they forget that to the young it is long.

"It is not the wisest of men who build palaces. The sages thought a roof to keep out the rain sufficient." Lord Zakoji lifted his teacup to his lips; the cup was even more lovely than those he had used on the journey.

"The cherry tree which we love to look at . . . its blossoms bear no fruits," he said and gazed searchingly at me.

I bent my head in agreement and said nothing.

When summer broke and the evenings were soft and the young bamboo shoots had grown long and bold, Lord Akiyama arranged some hunting parties. He took along young samurai of high rank, the sons of his captains; I, too, was invited. We would usually spend a couple of days on such expeditions, camping out at night and roasting some of the meat over open fires. Lord Akiyama had plenty of sake brought along and such parties were very merry, our master himself often being the most boisterous of all. Now that he was nearly a half hundred years old, he seemed to have acquired a taste for pursuits that more commonly please the young. He held archery contests, horse races, and wrestling matches and gave generous prizes to the winners. It was as if he had changed character, and the older samurai especially would discuss this endlessly without being able to find a reason that satisfied them. Once, as I was getting ready for such a hunting excursion, Wada Kansuke asked my opinion of the reason for the change in Lord Akiyama.

"It is his lady," I said with a laugh. "Our lord is in love with the wife he gained with the castle. Notice, too, that he dresses more like a young samurai than a lord and leader."

"Surely he has too much sense for that." Wada Kansuke gave me a sour look. "Love is for the young."

"A newly built house is slow to catch fire, whereas an old temple can go up in flames if the priests rub their prayer beads together too fast." I was looking forward to the hunt and enjoyed teasing my friend.

"One chop with an axe will cut a sapling in two," he admonished.

"A storm will fell the tallest tree in the forest and only bend the sapling," I rejoined.

"That is true." Wada Kansuke looked very serious, as if a new thought had suddenly struck him. "He knows, you see, that this will be the last summer for most of you, and so it pleases him to see you all happy. . . . Yes, that is the reason." The old samurai looked contented as he came to this explanation for his lord's behavior.

"That may be true," I said, for I was much too fond of Wada Kansuke to disagree with him. I realized that he had given to Lord Akiyama motives that would certainly have been his own had he been in his place.

"There is no doubt about it." Wada Kansuke chuckled at the thought. "He plays with you as a mother will play with a child before it is put to bed."

I had just slung my quiver full of arrows onto my back and was ready to go. The old samurai's words made me pause. "So you think that there will be no more summers for us?" I asked. I was in no doubt about the "bed" that my friend had referred to.

Wada Kansuke looked at me searchingly. "Death is the enemy we all have to face at some time or another. Does it matter when? You are a samurai, a warrior."

"It does matter when." The door to the outside was open; the brilliant sunshine of midday made the shadows short. "I would rather wait until it is evening to die." I grinned and then walked away, for I did not want to talk any more about death, I wanted to go hunting.

That evening as we sat around a fire in the mountains, Lord Akiyama was unusually silent. The others were boisterous; we had eaten a roasted wild pig and the jug of rice wine had been passed freely. Although I had tasted of it, I had drunk very little. I was sitting across from my lord when he waved to me, indicating that he wanted me to join him. I rose immediately and took a seat next to him.

"Can you remember, Taro, when you first saw me?" he asked.

"How could I forget that, sir? You spared my life," I answered, wondering why he had used my childhood name again.

"I am afraid that we shall need more than bamboo swords to spare our lives." Lord Akiyama was poking in the fire with a stick. Someone across from us had started to sing a song about sake. "Katsuyori has moved his army into Totomi to lay siege to Takatenjin Castle. He has asked me to send troops to his aid."

"He did not wait long," I said. "Is it because he lost Nagashino?" I asked.

Lord Akiyama shrugged his shoulders. "Who knows? He is too proud to take advice," he mumbled. "I wish that it had been he who ended his life in the temple, instead of Yoshinobu-sama. His brother had more sense; besides, through his mother he was related to the Heavenly Descended, whereas the Wakatono is a kept woman's child."

I nodded in agreement, for it was true that Katsuyori could not command the respect that was necessary to unite the Takeda army. To most of the samurai he was heir of the Suwa family, not of the Takedas.

"Is that why he wants to fight now," I asked, "while he still has command?"

"I wonder if he knows himself. . . ." Lord Akiyama threw the stick into the fire. "A man should be satisfied with this. To hunt in the mountains and then to return to his home, to a warm fire and good company." Lord Akiyama rose and stretched himself, then, looking down at me, he smiled. "Zakoji has talked of you. . . . He seems to want to adopt you. Well, I hope he has more luck than I have had in adopting sons. Mine all turn out sickly and dying. Maybe I should adopt you," he said teasingly, and when he saw the consternation on my face he laughed. "I shan't. . . . Zakoji has wealth to give that I cannot surpass." With these words he walked away and was swallowed up by the night. I remained staring into the leaping flames and dreamed of a future that did not contain even the shadow of death.

One thousand of our best warriors were sent to aid Katsuyori; among them was Yoshitoki. Wada Kansuke went along as officer in charge of the baggage train. I thought him too old for such a strenuous task and begged him that I should be sent in his stead. The last thing I wanted was to leave Iwamura Castle, but the old samurai had been like a father and I owed him a son's duty. However, he would not hear of it, and when I pressed him he grew angry. I asked Lord Zakoji to arrange for me to see Lord Akiyama. This was speedily done, but when I expressed my wish to take Wada Kansuke's place, Lord Akiyama laughed.

"You have strange luck, Harutomo; it is as if some god protects you. I had thought of sending you, but when your friend Kansuke heard of it he threatened me, saying that if you were sent he would take his own life." Lord Akiyama shook his head. "Well, in that case, I would have no-one to take charge of my stores, at least no-one I could trust. So I gave him what he desired, and now you come and make a demand that will make poor old Wada Kansuke commit seppuku. I cannot allow that. I thought there was something in Iwamura that kept you rooted like a tree to the place. Why do you want to leave?"

"I don't, sir," I blurted out, so moved that tears came into my eyes. "I thought it my duty, for he has been like a father to me."

"You seem to have an abundance of fathers." Lord

Akiyama grinned. "Go away with you, and don't bother me with nonsense like this." The last words were spoken in a gruff voice so I quickly bowed and took my leave.

In one day I lost both of those who had been closest to me, for I felt strongly that I should never see them again. Wada Kansuke left me in charge of all he owned. The old samurai was not rich. I was given his room in the castle, which was more spacious than my own little closet. The night before they left, the old samurai invited Yoshitoki to dine with us. This was not only because he was my friend, but Yoshitoki's presence would also keep Wada Kansuke from showing too plainly how much he cared for me. As we parted that night, Wada Kansuke put his hand on my shoulder and looked at me earnestly, as if he wished to draw a picture of me in his mind, then he pushed me gently away.

At first I had thought of riding along for part of the day with the departing army, but then I thought it better not to do so. Lord Akiyama had sent mostly cavalry to the aid of Katsuyori. This was because in the defense of Iwamura, should we be attacked, bowmen and foot soldiers would be of more use than the mounted men. The departing army looked splendid, their banners flying and their well-fed horses pawing the ground in eagerness to trot or gallop. The baggage train had the best of our animals, for it was important that they be able to keep up with the troops. From the top of Iwamura Castle I watched the departing soldiers until they disappeared from sight.

{ 29 }

Lord Zakoji Becomes a Priest

That winter the snow came early in the mountains, and the year ended in clear, frosty days. I had much work to do, for now I had Wada Kansuke's position. Lord Akiyama was concerned that the stores in the castle should be filled to overflowing, since he was expecting that Iwamura would be besieged. This meant that I had to make several trips through the district of Ina, collecting taxes and buying supplies. Takatenjin Castle had not fallen and none of the news we received from the army was promising. To prepare yourself for a siege is melancholy work, for it admits the possibility of defeat. The few times I saw Lord Akiyama he looked harassed; he no longer held archery competitions nor did he go hunting. Most of the time he spent in his quarters with his wife; once I heard her playing the zither. I had heard that she had a very pleasant voice.

Now that my friends had gone, I felt more bitterly alone. Even my love for Aki was no help, for her father seemed to have forgotten my existence. In desperation I sent her a poem.

The sickle moon has left the sky;
Mount Fuji's snow is winter deep.
I fear that spring shall never come
As, all alone, I long for you.

I did not receive an answer to my poem, and when I sent a further letter, it was answered not by Aki but by a note from her father. He asked me to come to his room immediately. I was greatly surprised on entering to see that his head was shaven and that he was dressed in the robes of a priest.

"I have decided to spend my last days preparing myself for the next world," he said, looking at me severely. "If we should be spared, I wish to live in a hermitage in the mountains as far away from the world and its temptation as I can get."

"We have not lost yet. Katsuyori may still lead his army to victory," I muttered.

"I sincerely hope so, and I shall pray for his victory. But I doubt if it will happen," Lord Zakoji sighed. He occupied a room in the upper castle, and the paper screen was drawn so one could see out over the valley below. "Soon there will be a battle and, if Katsuyori loses, it will be the last battle that the Takeda armies will fight."

I nodded in agreement.

"If Katsuyori is defeated, we shall either die or have to make peace with Oda Nobunaga. That is, if he is willing to spare us or should find it to his advantage."

"And can we trust his word?" I asked.

"Will we have any choice but to trust him?" Lord Zakoji looked out over the valley as if he could already see the Oda armies marching toward our castle.

"I do not know, sir. Lord Katsuyori has not lost any battle yet." I could not help thinking that Lord Zakoji's attitude was not one worthy of a samurai.

"The priest's robe does not mean that I cannot bend a bow or wield a sword if the need should arise." Lord Zakoji smiled as if he had guessed my thoughts. "I called you here to ask you not to write any more letters to my daughter. I wish her to spend her time in prayer to Lord Buddha rather than replying to poems from Prince Genji." The last words were a real affront, for they referred to the *Tale of Genji*, a book that I had heard of but never read. It was written a long time ago and was about the love affairs of a prince.

"My poems were clumsy, I know," I said, my face growing red as I realized that Lord Zakoji had read all my poems. "They must have seemed foolish and childish to you."

"No, they are not bad." Aki's father smiled. "If we live, I shall yet call you my son. Those who have not written poems in their youth will not be able to pray in their old age. I only ask of you that you refrain from writing until I tell you that you may again unleash the waning moon, willow trees, and misty mornings upon my daughter."

"I shall obey you," I said and, bowing, I left.

On the way back to my own quarters I met Lord Akiyama. As I bowed deeply and stood still to let him pass, he stopped and asked where I had come from. When I told him that I had been visiting Lord Zakoji he smiled, and for a moment his features looked youthful as he said, "And how does his new habit strike you? I think his head must be cold without any hair."

"He seems much concerned about the next world," I

muttered, for it is unwise to laugh too loudly when one lord makes fun of another. "He has asked his daughter to pray for Lord Katsuyori to win a victory."

"I have heard that she is supposed to spend her time in prayer." Realizing what this meant to me, he added, "Do not worry, the girl is fond of you — so she has confided to my wife. In good time I shall talk to Zakoji and be your go-between."

I bowed and thanked him, being much honored by this proposal. Lord Akiyama nodded and walked on; he still wore his silk kimono, but his swords were in his sash.

Although the winter was severe, spring came early. Suddenly all the brooks started singing as the waters from the melting snow rushed down into the valleys. I was kept busy and spent most of my time with the men of the Konidatai and with my servant, Yoichi. Without him I would have been very lonely, for I could talk to him without fear of being thought foolish, and I kept few secrets from him.

In a small village two days' march from Iwamura, I learned of Takeda Katsuyori's great defeat. He had captured Takatenjin Castle and this victory had made him rashly push on to recapture Nagashino, but there his army had been vanquished and totally destroyed. Of its generals and officers not a handful was left. When he heard the news, Lord Akiyama immediately sent a messenger to recall me to the castle, knowing full well that the armies of Oda Nobunaga would now turn on Iwamura.

We walked day and night, resting only when the men

and packhorses were exhausted. As we entered the valley of Iwamura, I feared that we should see the enemy armies already encamped. But everything was peaceful as we made our way through the village; the frightened expressions on the faces of the people told me that they already knew. As soon as we entered the castle gate, I left Yoichi to take the supplies to the stores and rushed to tell Lord Akiyama that I had returned. Strangely, he seemed more at ease than he had been for a long time. It was as if he had regained his spirit now that he knew that all was lost. As I left him he quoted a line from a prayer:

"In the raging fire of this world there is no peace."

{30}

The Siege of Iwamura Castle

"Look!" a young samurai exclaimed as he pointed down into the valley. "They are choosing the same site for their headquarters as Lord Akiyama did."

"It is a good place." From the top of the ramparts of the castle we were watching the huge Oda army taking possession of the valley, and I was thinking that from here they looked like an army of ants. "Is Oda Nobunaga himself there, I wonder?" I asked.

"I think his son Nobutada is in command; I recognize his banner." The young samurai was still peering down at the little hillock about an arrow's flight from the castle gate where their headquarters was being established.

"Were you at Nagashino?" I asked, suddenly recognizing the young man as a comrade of Yoshitoki. I knew that Wada Kansuke had died in that battle and I had prayed for the repose of his soul with more fervor than I had ever prayed to Buddha before. But the fate of Yoshitoki I had yet to learn.

"It was not a battle, we were slaughtered." For a moment the young warrior closed his eyes as if he wanted to imagine the battle again. "Again and again we attacked, until there was no-one left. They had guns, several hundred of them, and a piked barricade from behind which they could shoot at us at their leisure. It was like a whole army committing seppuku. The horses that were not killed by the bullets got so frightened that one could hardly handle them; mine shook as if it had been beaten."

"You were with Yoshitoki?" I asked, fearing what I was going to hear.

"He was killed in the very first attack. I saw him fall from his horse." The young samurai turned his gaze away from me down toward the valley. "He was your friend?" he asked.

I nodded for I could not speak; I felt tears forming in my eyes. I looked away and managed to ask my companion, "Why did you keep attacking? Would it not have been better to retreat?"

"Each time, Lord Katsuyori ordered us to attack again. . . . It was as if he could no longer give any other order. He watched us as we galloped past, his father's war-fan in his hand."

"The Wakatono. . . ." I smiled bitterly; somehow I had hoped that by some miracle Yoshitoki might still be alive. Now I saw him falling from his horse to the dust below.

"It was not only Lord Katsuyori, but the rest of us, too, who had gone mad. We wanted to charge exactly that impregnable place in their lines." The young samurai smiled as if the memory of that bloody day was somehow pleasant for him. "We had found the gate of the road to the west, the gate to death, and we were as eager to pass through it as if it were the gate of a palace and we the guests invited to a feast."

"How many died?" I asked. From the plain below I

heard the sound of a soldier blowing a conch shell, trumpeting some message or another.

"Most of the lords; of all the generals of Lord Takeda Shingen, no more than you could count on the fingers of one hand remain. As for the ordinary bushi, for every five who entered the battle, I doubt if one is still alive." The young samurai stood up, stretched himself, and left me. I stayed for a while, thinking of Yoshitoki and Wada Kansuke, promising myself that I would have services said for them in the temple of Erin-ji if I left Iwamura alive.

Although the Oda army was so large that there were twenty warriors for every one of ours, they were in no hurry to attack us. It was now proven how wise Lord Akiyama had been in keeping the best archers in the castle. A few days before the arrival of our enemies, he had had bushes and trees cut down within an arrow's flight of the walls of the castle so that there was no cover from which they could shoot at us. The Oda army had guns, but they were not very accurate at a great distance and, with our best bowmen placed at intervals along the wall, none of the Oda soldiers seemed eager to venture into the open land.

Since I was in charge of the storehouse, I had many meetings with Lord Akiyama and his staff of older, high-ranking samurai. We had water in plenty and food for the first six months at least. When Lord Akiyama had cleared the land around the castle, he had also sent away most of the women and children and those so elderly that they would be of no use.

Strangely enough, I think that the younger samurai especially suffered most from boredom. Iwamura Castle comprises an entire small mountain, but once you are locked within its walls, it does not seem so large. In secret, a group planned a foray. About fifty young samurai assembled early one morning near the lower gate, mounted on the best of our horses. When the gate was opened they charged out and, with wild shouts, galloped through the enemy camp. But the Oda forces were prepared. The general allowed them to break through his lines, but when they wished to return a host of Oda soldiers followed them. By that time Lord Akiyama had been warned of what had happened. He ordered the gate to be closed, and we watched the fifty young soldiers being slaughtered. Later, their heads were exhibited on pikes near the Oda headquarters for us to contemplate as our own likely fate.

After a meeting with his staff that I had been asked to attend in order to inform them of the remaining supplies, Lord Akiyama asked me to stay. He invited me to sit down and ordered tea to be brought; then he changed his mind and ordered sake instead.

"Taro," he said as he lifted his cup, "may you be as lucky with Oda Nobunaga as you were years ago with Takeda Shingen!"

"May I never need to be," I rejoined.

"If . . ." Lord Akiyama shook his head as if he did not believe what he was going to say. "If Katsuyori managed to build up yet another Takeda army and attacked Oda Nobutada here in the valley of Iwamura, he might possibly win. But he would have to come swiftly and secretly before Nobutada's father brings the rest of the army."

"How many soldiers does Nobutada have?" I asked.

"Fifteen thousand, maybe a few more, but if we attacked at the same time as Katsuyori, there would be some hope. In any case, I would like to know what Katsuyori's plans are." Lord Akiyama took the little pitcher that had been placed near him and filled our cups again. "I want to send a messenger to Kofuchu while we still are strong enough to be of some value."

"It should be some samurai of high rank," I suggested. "Someone Lord Katsuyori would trust."

"The older men that are with me are all friends of Katsuyori's father. They look upon him as a child and, as I call you 'Taro,' they may forget themselves and call him by his boyhood name, 'Shiro.' No, they will not do. . . . I have heard that Katsuyori only keeps council with samurai his own age. Besides, I need someone who has the cunning of a ninja and will be able to escape from Iwamura Castle and pass through the Oda army without being caught." Lord Akiyama paused and I blushed, because only now did I understand what he was suggesting. "Do you think you can do it?"

"I can try," I answered and frowned. "I shall do my best."

"If they catch you they will crucify you — that is what Oda Nobunaga usually does with ninjas." Lord Akiyama was toying with his little sake cup.

"I am not afraid of dying." As I spoke those words I meant them, for the young do not fear death.

{31}

I Leave Iwamura Castle

I spent a great deal of time on the ramparts of the castle, scrutinizing the land below. I wanted to be able to recall, in the depths of the night, every hillock and every tree or bush that grew in the valley. I was planning to leave on the first cloudy, moonless night and had gotten a cloak as black as any ninja ever wore. Although I was busy preparing myself for the task that Lord Akiyama had ordered me to accomplish, my thoughts would often return to Lord Zakoji's daughter, Aki. I had obeyed her father and had not written to her, but several times I had seen her and our eyes had spoken, although we had been mute. Finally, when the weather seemed to be changing and the moon was new, I decided to ask my servant, Yoichi, to try to arrange a meeting between us.

Part of the upper castle was occupied by Lady Akiyama and her attendants, and they walked on the ramparts on fair days. There, I was told, Aki-hime would be waiting for me in the hour of the ram. Should anyone see us it would look like mere chance that we had met. The hour of the horse had not yet passed when I eagerly began keeping watch. Hiding behind a wall I could see the stretch of the ramparts where we were to meet. It was the middle of the hour of the ram when she came. At first I almost ran, but then I remembered that we were meeting by chance and walked slowly towards her. When she saw me she turned her face away and stood looking at the valley below. Until I said her name I did not realize that we had never spoken to each other before. From the notes and poems that had passed between us, I felt that we knew each other well. Yet now, when I could speak to her for the first time, I grew confused and muttered something about leaving soon. Turning to me and covering half of her face with the sleeve of her kimono, she answered that she had heard so from her father and that she would pray for my success. I smiled and thanked her, and there we stood staring at each other like two fools who have not the wit to speak. Suddenly Aki laughed and blushed, then I laughed too and my face grew red. Then words tumbled from my mouth. I told her that I would come back and that I would protect her and a thousand other things that all meant that I loved her and that would sound foolish if written down. While I spoke, Aki stood with her head bent. When I had finished she looked at me for a moment and smiled. With tears in her eyes, she turned and ran toward the part of the castle where she lived. She was like a little bird, I thought, who had dared to venture down on the ground and now flew back into the safety of the trees.

As the hour of the ram drew to a close, banks of cloud rose in the east, promising rain and bad weather. Perhaps because I had spoken to Aki-hime and felt sure that she cared for me, I decided to ask Lord Akiyama for permission to leave Iwamura that very night. Just as the black clouds swallowed up the evening sun, I was told to come to Lord Akiyama's room.

To my surprise, I was not shown into the room that Lord Akiyama normally used but into a smaller one. As I entered, he looked up and motioned me to sit down near him. Lord Akiyama was seated by a desk with ink and brushes nearby; he had obviously just finished writing.

"Here are two letters. One is for my father — deliver that first. Then take this one — " Lord Akiyama pointed to a rolled up letter tied with a purple string — "and give it to Lord Katsuyori. Give it into his hands, not to one of his retainers." Lord Akiyama lifted the letter and looked at it. "It will gain me little, I fear, for I am sure I could write the reply too. Still, one must do things according to custom. Here!"

I reached out and took the letters, then tucked them away in my sleeve. "I shall deliver them," I said. At my words, a fleeting smile appeared on Lord Akiyama's face.

"If, contrary to my expectations, Takeda Katsuyori will come to my aid, have a fire lit in the mountains that we may see it clearly." Lord Akiyama turned towards the back of the room where a sliding door was partly open. "Everyone must fight a last battle before he dies. It is bitter to say good-bye to life when the blood in your veins still gushes like a river in June, Taro. Yet one must strive to pass out of this world with dignity." Behind the screen I thought I heard a slight rustle of silk against silk. Lady Akiyama is there, listening, I thought, and he knows it.

"No-one has ever laughed at me to my face. Behind my back they may have called me a wild buffalo and thought me foolish, with little more sense than that animal has." Lord Akiyama paused and a bitter smile crossed his face. "Takeda Shingen called me Haruchika. He was my friend, and I shall be loyal to his son. For if all sense of loyalty is gone, what will happen then? Sometimes I think that it is melting fast like last year's snow."

"But, my lord," I objected, "if we are to be loyal, have we not the right to demand loyalty from those whom we serve?"

"Should we demand loyalty from the Emperor before we would serve him? Like a shopkeeper in the market who asks for payment before he will hand over his wares?"

I shook my head. I wanted to say that Takeda Katsuyori was not the Emperor of Japan, but I did not dare.

Lord Akiyama looked down at the dirk that was stuck in his sash. "I could never shave my head, Taro." Although Lord Akiyama spoke my name, his face was turned towards the half-opened door. "I would make a poor priest — I could lead no-one towards Buddha. A priest's robe may hide a sword, but I shall wear mine openly to the last. I do not wish to die!" Lord Akiyama sighed. "Especially now. . . . Sometimes an old cherry tree will flower more beautifully than one that is young. Its tender blossoms will hide its gnarled branches." A sound like a sob came from behind the screen, and Lord Akiyama turned almost angrily toward me. "You have heard me," he said. "Now, be on your way!"

"I will, my lord," I mumbled in my embarrassment. I

rose to go, but before I had reached the door, Lord Akiyama called out, "Harutomo!"

Obediently, I turned. Lord Akiyama was smiling.

"Taro, my lord," I said as I thought, That is how he looks when he smiles to her, to the lady behind the screen.

"To me, yes, you are Taro. It is the name I gave you long ago. But to everyone else you are Murakami Harutomo, one of my most trusted retainers." Lord Akiyama lifted his hand as a sign of my dismissal. I bowed and left. I never saw him alive again.

I planned to leave in the night when the hour of the rat was over. It was raining hard and was as dark as I could wish. I was dressed totally in black and had smeared soot on my face. I had even allowed my teeth to be blackened. I had kept the secret of my departure from everyone; only my servant knew. I carried Lord Akiyama's letters in a leather bag around my neck. Although my swords were cumbersome, I wore them. Yoichi was heartbroken to see me leave and begged to be allowed to accompany me.

There was a secret exit from the castle, but I feared that it was not as secret as some believed, so I decided to descend on a rope at a place on the wall that was not heavily guarded below. Here, too, a few bushes and trees grew fairly close to the wall. These would make it easier to hide. I fastened the rope to a rock jutting out from the top of the rampart and then let it down. The last human face I saw in Iwamura Castle was Yoichi's as I climbed down into the darkness.

{32}

Takeda Katsuyori

When I let go of the rope, the darkness of the night engulfed me. As swiftly as I dared, I moved down to where I knew I would find some bushes to hide among. There I stayed for a while to accustom my eyes to the darkness. As I was now on the opposite side of the mountain from the valley and the road that leads to Kofuchu, I had to make my way around the base of the mountain castle. It was raining hard and I was sure that no-one could see me, but once I dislodged a stone and a voice shouted, "Who goes there?" I lay as still as a mouse and a little while later I heard someone declare that it was probably a horse that had broken loose.

It was important that I should have traveled out of the valley by sunrise, so I gave myself no rest. When the first glimmering of dawn came, I was in the foothills of the mountains. I washed my face in a stream and ate the rice-balls I had brought with me. It was still raining, and I was drenched through.

Since it was the tenth month of the year, the sun rose late and the dark clouds made it a dreary morning that few would venture out in. I walked as fast as I could, keeping to the road, until I met a path that I knew led to a charcoal burner's hut. Here lived a family whom I had befriended and had bought charcoal from. My plan was to spend the daylight hours with them, and then, as soon as night fell once more, to make my way to Iida Castle, where I could obtain a horse. I was made welcome and was given warm food and a place near the brazier.

When night came the oldest of the sons decided to accompany me to Iida. He loaded their horse with bags of charcoal and I hid my swords among them. Then he gave me a straw raincoat and a peasant hat in place of my black cloak and we set out, two sellers of charcoal should we meet any of Oda's soldiers. We met no-one, and in the early morning we arrived at Iida. Here the governor of the castle lent me clothes and a horse. I stayed only as long as politeness required, and by noon I was on my way. At the gate of the castle I saw my companion from the previous night; he hailed me, saying that he had a message for me from his father. The old charcoal burner wanted to let me know that if I were ever in trouble and needed help, I should come to him. I told the son to thank his father, little knowing that it would not be long before I was to take advantage of this offer.

I gave myself no rest and my horse no more than it needed in order to carry me. Even so, near Kofuchu I almost had a fall. I was half asleep and the horse stumbled from exhaustion. In the early morning I rode into Lord Akiyama's mansion. The stars had faded and the outline of the mountains was stark as if it had been painted with a brush on the ivory sky. I put the horse into the stable, and, since no-one seemed to be awake, I took the time to rub down the poor beast. When I had finished, the mountaintops had turned pale pink, yet no-one was stirring. I walked to the cookhouse where I had lived as a boy and, sitting under the tree where Togan and I used to spend so many summer evenings, I tried to recall his features. But it was too cold to sit dreaming under trees and I soon rose. A young boy came from the cookhouse carrying a bucket; he had been sent for water. He bowed humbly as he passed me and I could not help smiling and wondering if he, too, dreamed of becoming a samurai.

When some of the servants stirred in the main house I asked them to tell Lord Akiyama's father that I had come, bringing a message from his son. I expected to be kept waiting, but the old samurai was eager to hear news and I was led to his room almost immediately. He looked as vigorous as ever; age seemed to dry rather than bend him. He ordered the servant to bring breakfast for us both and told me to sit down opposite him. I gave him his son's letter. He unrolled it and held it almost at arm's length while he read. When he had finished, he carefully rolled it again and put it in his sleeve.

"Tell me," the old lord smiled, "is she beautiful?" Noticing the confusion painted on my face he added, "My son's new wife."

"I have been told that she is, but I have never seen her. I once heard her play the zither and that sounded very beautiful," I said.

"She can sing and play the zither." The old samurai nodded in approval. "When my son was young, I once tried to have him taught to play the flute, but I am afraid he had little talent."

"It is most difficult to play it well," I agreed, for I, too, had once tried to master that instrument.

"I understand you have been sent with a message from my son to Katsuyori." The old man frowned as the servants entered with two little tables containing our morning meal. I merely nodded, not wishing to speak while they were present.

As soon as the servants had left I said, "Lord Akiyama wants his letter to be given to — " I caught my breath, for I had almost said "the Wakatono," but managed to blurt out "Lord Katsuyori" instead.

Almost imperceptibly, the old samurai smiled. "You mean it is to be given into his hands, not to one of his followers?"

"Lord Akiyama is afraid that if they see it first it may never reach Lord Katsuyori."

"I shall send someone to the castle saying that you have come, and that you bear a message for Takeda Katsuyori from my son." Lord Akiyama's father was picking with his chopsticks at the fish in front of him rather than eating it. Hungrily I had already devoured mine. "How long can my son hold the castle?"

"We have food for another month at least." I looked down at the empty dishes in front of me. "But they are at least fifteen to every one of us. If Katsuyori will come, I am to light a fire in the mountain. That fire will kindle more than wood for those inside Iwamura Castle. If no help comes, then . . ." I shrugged my shoulders.

"Then you can be glad that you, at least, escaped," Lord Akiyama's father muttered.

"Whatever message Lord Katsuyori has for me to bring my master, I shall deliver," I said almost angrily, for I took the old man's words as a reflection upon my honor.

"It was easier to leave Iwamura than it will be to get back," he countered. "But go and rest, for you must be tired. I shall send someone to see the Oyakata-sama."

I rose, bowing to the old samurai as I left. A servant showed me to a room and put out bedding for me on the floor. Soon, in a dream, I was back in Iwamura Castle.

I thought that I had just fallen asleep when someone woke me. To my surprise, it was past noon and well into the hour of the ram. A messenger had arrived from Tsutsujigasaki Castle, bidding me to go there. I was pleased that I had been called so soon, for I thought it showed Lord Katsuyori's interest in the fate of Iwamura. All the way to the castle I daydreamed about firing a beacon in the mountains, sending the good news to my master and my friends. I thought too of how proud Akihime would be of me and how much closer such an act would bring me to the fulfillment of my desires.

As I was led into the big council room, I was in high spirits. Takeda Katsuyori was seated on a little platform, and beside him sat several young samurai.

One of them took the letter from my hand and gave it to Lord Katsuyori, who unrolled and read it. When he had finished he handed it to the samurai who sat nearest to him. Then, turning his gaze towards me, he asked, "How long can the castle hold?"

"If they receive news that help will come, then at least two months. Left without hope, I think less. There is food for at least a month and that can be stretched to last longer."

"And how many troops do you guess that the Oda army consists of?"

"They are fifteen or twenty to every one of us." I watched Lord Akiyama's letter being passed around as I spoke. "We are a little more than a thousand, but better soldiers than they."

At my last words, Lord Katsuyori smiled disdainfully. Shortly afterwards I was dismissed and told that I would be called when the Oyakata-sama had decided what answer to send. All the hopes that had made me step so light-heartedly on my way to the castle were now gone. I felt certain that I would not be lighting any beacons of hope to the besieged in Iwamura Castle.

{33}

The Ninja Again

I expected to be called to the castle the next day, but no messenger came. The old Lord Akiyama, who did not usually care much for company, had me in attendance most of the time. He was known as a very fine archer who, when younger, had won all the competitions among the samurai of Kai. Now he took charge of me to teach me. I was honored by his attention, although I realized it was partly because he could talk to me about his son. Lord Akiyama had obviously been the favorite among his children, and he was very proud of him. I told him about our hunting expeditions the previous summer and, naturally, about our first meeting and how his son had taken charge of me. One day we rode to the townland of Haruchika where there was a small castle and a shrine belonging to Lord Akiyama. It was pleasant to be with the old man, but, as days went by without hearing anything from the castle, we both grew worried. The old samurai attempted to see Takeda Katsuyori but was told that Lord Takeda was occupied and had no time to spare. He returned to his own house in a furious temper, for he was a man who cared passionately about his dignity and the young samurai had dismissed him as if he were some itinerant priest who had come begging. The sickle moon had grown full and started to wane again, yet we heard nothing. When I finally learned of Lord Katsuyori's decision, it was not from him.

I had been wandering around the town when I spied a person whom I thought I knew going into a sake shop. The area around the market is not the best; it is said to be dangerous once the sun has set. But since this was early in the afternoon and the hour of the ram was not yet over, I followed the man. When I entered the sake shop, he had already seated himself and was being served by a young girl. I looked at him sharply. I knew that I had seen him before, yet I could not recall where. I guessed he was a poor bushi, not a samurai of great importance. Suddenly I remembered; he was the ninja I had met that night in front of Iwamura Castle. Obviously he, too, was wondering who I was. Suddenly he smiled and motioned me to sit down.

"We have met before, but I cannot remember where," he said.

"You were dressed differently then," I replied, seating myself and ordering the girl to bring me some warm sake. "It was below Iwamura Castle. . . . You had just returned from it. I was with Wada Kansuke and another friend."

"How strange." The ninja lifted his sake cup in a silent toast. "I have just come from there again."

I felt my heart beat faster as I asked, as though it were no great concern of mine, "Why were you there?"

"I brought a message to its governor from Lord Takeda. There are as many Oda soldiers surrounding it as there are ants in an anthill." The ninja filled his sake cup once more.

"Will they be able to hold out much longer?" I asked, trying to sound as if I did not care what happened.

"He was told to try to come to some kind of agreement with Oda Nobunaga — the castle for their lives." The ninja had emptied his little pitcher of sake and I ordered another. "Lord Takeda is willing to give up the castle — which they cannot hold for long anyway — if he can save the soldiers, for he is in greater need of them."

"Is Oda Nobunaga there? I thought it was his son, Nobutada, who was in command." To my disgust, I realized that my hand betrayed me. As I lifted my sake cup it trembled.

"Lord Nobunaga is there. He came only a few days ago; I saw his banner flying where they have their headquarters." The ninja smiled a little. "You are very interested in Iwamura Castle."

"I have friends there." I poured some sake into my own cup. "Will Nobunaga grant them safe conduct to leave?"

The ninja shook his head. "I would not care to bargain with Oda Nobunaga; his stall in the marketplace is not one a ninja would go near."

I suddenly recalled that Oda Nobunaga hated the ninjas and had them killed whenever he caught one.

"Lord Akiyama's wife is Oda's aunt," I commented.

"She married your master without her nephew's permission. I doubt if he will forgive her that." The ninja emptied his sake cup and rose. "You are the messenger who came here from Iwamura," he stated rather than asked. I nodded. The ninja smiled, patted the hilts of his swords, and left. Only after the door had closed behind him did I realize that he had left the payment for all the sake he had drunk to me.

I ran as quickly as I could to Lord Akiyama's mansion. Once there, I searched for his father and found him practicing archery in the garden. When I told him what had happened, he handed his bow to a servant and motioned me to follow him inside.

"Why did Katsuyori send the ninja and not you?" The old samurai frowned and then answered his own question. "Because he did not trust you. Yes, that must have been the reason."

"I think the ninja knew from the very start that he was talking to Lord Akiyama's messenger. What he told me may not be the truth," I suggested.

"You might have told my son too much of what you have seen here."

"I shall leave for Iwamura right away," I declared. "I fear that Lord Katsuyori may forbid me to return."

"You are loyal to my son. Go saddle my best horse and be ready! I shall write a letter for you to take."

As I saddled the horse, I wondered if, had Aki not been in Iwamura Castle, I would have been so eager to return. As I led the horse from the stable, I feared all the time that a messenger would come from Tsutsujigasaki Castle, ordering me to go there. I debated with myself if I should dare disobey such an order, but, happily, no messenger came.

"Here!" Lord Akiyama Nobutora handed me a letter, and I put it away in the same pouch that had contained his son's letter to Takeda Katsuyori on my way to Kofuchu. "Tell him . . ." The old samurai looked around him, then bit his lip and said no more. He handed me a leather purse while he mumbled, "For the journey. . . ." I spurred my horse, for I saw that a tear had formed in the old man's eye and was running down his furrowed cheek.

Again, I rode as if I wished to kill my horse, and, once more, it proved itself as sturdy an animal as I have ever sat astride. I did not rest until I was once more inside Iida Castle. There I left my mount, the poor beast trembling like an aspen leaf. I do not think it could have carried me much farther. The governor of the castle made me stay the night. The next morning I set out again, planning to head for the charcoal burner's cottage and there to change my clothes and leave my horse. The beast I was given at Iida was a mare that saw no reason for haste. By the time I reached the path leading to the cottage, darkness had fallen and I almost missed my way. The house seemed very dark, and I called out a greeting. Soon a light appeared and one of the daughters came and took my horse. The charcoal burner had only one small oil lamp, which shed a poor light, so I could not see the expression on his face as I said that I was on my way to Iwamura.

"Iwamura," he repeated and indicated for me to sit

down beside the brazier and warm myself. "Have you not heard?" he asked.

"I have heard nothing from the castle since I left." I held my hands over the warm coals.

"Iwamura Castle has fallen. The banner of Oda Nobunaga now flies from its battlements."

The girl who had taken my horse entered silently and kneeled near me.

"And did Lord Oda give my master freedom to leave?" My voice shook, for I knew what the answer would be.

"Yes." The charcoal burner looked into my face as if he wanted to judge exactly how I would take the news. "Lord Oda made them leave on the road to the west. . . . He killed them all, though he had promised them their lives."

"Everyone?" I clenched my hands so hard that I could feel the nails bite into my palms.

"Even the women and children. He had Lord Akiyama and three others crucified, as if they were common criminals."

"And what happened to his aunt, Lady Akiyama, and the women who served her?"

"Dead! They say that Oda himself cut off her head. The swords of his samurai grew blunt from overwork. Down by his headquarters they piled up heads like vegetables ready for the market."

"May I borrow some clothing from your sons? The meanest kind — I will go to Iwamura."

"I will lend you whatever you want. I'll give you a bag of charcoal to carry on your back; it will serve as the best disguise. But I would rather you stayed here. . . . I told you that in Iwamura they are all dead. Remain with us. . . ." The old charcoal burner gave a nod in the direction of his daughter. "If you stay here you will need nothing; she will make as good a wife as anyone you will find in Kofuchu."

"I must go to Iwamura," I repeated, although at that moment I felt so tired that I could hardly move.

"When?" The old man stirred the coals in the brazier.

"Very soon. I only need to rest a while."

"Stay!" The old charcoal burner held up a hand to stop my protest. "Your master is dead and cannot any longer demand from you that you should follow him. The young rush to the road to the west as if they were sure of being reborn as princes. You are not a child any longer. Stay here!"

I smiled bitterly. He was right, I was not a child anymore; my youth was over. I thanked the old man, for he meant it kindly, and told him that I would be back. I did not tell him that I could not live there in the dark forest. I smiled at the girl and she smiled back. In the mirror of her eyes, I saw my own image reflected — a young samurai — and I wondered if it had been she who had begged her father to ask me to stay.

{34}

The End of the Tale

When I finally left the charcoal burner's hut, I was wearing rags fit for my lowly position, and on my back I carried a bag of charcoal. The old man wanted to cut my hair to suit my clothing, but I would not let him. I was wearing the kind of broad hat that peasants wear and I hoped that no-one would ask me to remove it, for underneath my hair was still cut and dressed in the manner of a samurai. It would have been wiser to have chopped my hair as if it had been done by my wife or mother in the village I came from, but I could not. Even then I could not let go of that rank that it had caused me so much hardship to achieve.

As I came nearer to the valley I met some of Oda Nobunaga's soldiers. They did not notice me as I stepped to the side of the road to let them pass. Two of them were laughing; they were as gay and carefree as soldiers are when they have been victorious. When I entered the valley and could see the castle for the first time, nothing seemed to have changed. It was almost noon, the hour of the horse, when I entered the village.

The town had spread since the Oda army had come; new shacks had been built to house those who live by following an army. As I passed a shop, the owner hailed me and asked the price of my charcoal. I told him what I wanted for it. The shopkeeper immediately paid the sum, and I bowed humbly and put away the copper coins he gave me. It was a relief not to carry the sack of charcoal, although my disguise was now less perfect. A samurai has a typical way of striding, whereas peasants often shuffle their feet rather than lifting them as they walk. Now that I no longer carried the burden of charcoal, I would have to be twice as careful.

I made my way to the hillock that had been Oda Nobutada's headquarters. I did not want to see my master Lord Akiyama's crucified body and hoped that it had been removed. It had not! Four crosses had been erected; one of them leaned as if it were about to fall. The four bodies were naked; they had been placed upside down on the crosses in the same manner as criminals were crucified. Lord Akiyama was the first, and next to him hung the body of Aki's father, Lord Zakoji. Shaving his head and becoming a Buddhist priest had not saved him from this miserable end. Somehow the corpses looked more like grotesque dolls than bodies that had once contained souls.

"He did not suffer long," said a voice close to me. I turned and saw a man standing near me. "I was allowed to kill them almost as soon as they were put up. He was very brave," the man said, pointing to Lord Akiyama.

"What happened to his wife?" I asked. I knew it was custom to kill whoever was crucified by sticking a spear into them. "Was she crucified too?"

"No." The man shook his head. "They say that she was killed by her nephew, but I don't know if that is true.

Her head is over there among the others." He pointed to a row of heads, which stared blindly in death. "We have been ordered to bury them all tomorrow." Then, with a certain amount of pride, he added, "There are more of them, but these are all the important ones."

I walked over and glanced at Lady Akiyama's head. Even now I could see that she had been beautiful. Next to her were the heads of some of the ladies who had served her. I hardly dared look, but Aki was not among them. To kill a man who stands in your way to power will always be done, but to humiliate even the dead body of your enemy is shameful. Oda Nobunaga had crucified his own honor rather than Lord Akiyama's. Forgetting myself, I stood in front of his cross and prayed that Lord Buddha would give him peace and that if he were to be reborn it would be as a prince. Then I bowed deeply for the last time to the master I had served and walked away.

I was lucky that none of Oda's soldiers were nearby, for surely I had not behaved like a curious peasant but more like what I was — a retainer of Lord Akiyama who had come to pay his last respects to his chief. I wondered if in the village I might find some survivor who could tell me what had been the fate of my servant Yoichi and of Aki-hime. The thought that one or both of them might have escaped did not occur to me.

"Master," a voice whispered. I was standing among a crowd, watching some wandering priests who had set up their altar in the street and were now ready to tell the fortune of anyone gullible enough to give them a coin or two. It was Yoichi; he stood next to me, a wide grin splitting his mouth and showing his stumps of teeth. "Follow me, master," he said.

On the outskirts of the village, in front of a dilapidated shack, he stopped. "In there, master," he said, pointing to the opening, which was closed not by a door but by a mat. I pushed the roughly woven mat aside and stepped over the threshold. At first I thought the hut was empty, but then I spied what I took to be a boy crouching in a corner.

"Who are you?" I demanded, stepping nearer and putting my hand on the youth's head to turn it. It was not a boy, it was Aki-hime!

"Aki-hime," I said softly. The girl shook her head and held her hands in front of her face.

"Only Aki, a girl who has no parents," she whispered. Then looking up at me she said, "The night before we left the castle, my father burned the letters and papers he had, and I burned your poems and letters too. Now it is as if they had never been written."

I grasped her hand and forced her to stand up. She looked down at her clothes — a ragged paper kimono that would scarcely serve to hide a servant girl's nakedness.

"I am not worthy now of any man," she sighed.

"Look at me," I said and smiled, pointing to my own rags. "We will make a fine couple."

For a moment a smile lit her face. Her hair had been cut short, but I thought it only made her prettier.

That night the three of us, I — Murakami Harutomo — Aki-hime, and Yoichi, made our way through the army of Oda Nobunaga, and some days later we arrived safely in Kofuchu.

The story of a man's life ends only when death makes the final brush-stroke, but with the fall of Iwamura Castle and the death of my master, Lord Akiyama Nobutomo, ended my youth. The tale of the parentless child and the young samurai has been told. What happened later may also be worth the telling, for honor demanded that I attempt to avenge my master. The prayer says that "in the raging fire of the world, there is no peace." Yet that is not altogether true, for in the love between two human beings that fire can be quenched and peace may be found.